THE LONE
MISSIONARY

EDDIE RAINBOLT

WestBow
PRESS®
A DIVISION OF THOMAS NELSON
& ZONDERVAN

WestBow Press books may be ordered through booksellers or by contacting:

WestBow Press
A Division of Thomas Nelson & Zondervan
1663 Liberty Drive
Bloomington, IN 47403
www.westbowpress.com
1 (866) 928-1240

ISBN: 978-1-9736-9434-2 (sc)
ISBN: 978-1-9736-9433-5 (e)

Print information available on the last page.

WestBow Press rev. date: 6/15/2020

1

I saw it coming. She warned she was leaving. I just didn't accept it. We'd been together for ten years. I was here first but we were a good fit. She complemented me in every way. We weren't married but we worked together like a happily married couple. But we didn't fight like it. We got along together just like we should have. But she announced to me she was going and when.

It was during one of our prayer sessions that she felt like she needed to break the news. I heard her say something in her prayer about her time remaining. I was floored at first. I wondered at her meaning. I thought she said something about leaving, so I asked.

She replied, "I'm afraid so. It's a budget thing. They can't budget for two of us here. So, since you have tenure, I have to leave…"

She trailed off as she said it. I could tell there was more.

I said, "I feel like there's possibly more to this than you're telling me."

She looked away, maybe to avoid hurting me with something. But she looked back and me and spoke.

She said, "It's all money. There's a chance they'll be closing the mission."

I admit I became comfortable here to the point I thought I'd be here forever. I never suspected they'd close the place. But, nothing lasts forever, does it? It seemed she felt guilty for telling me.

"Why do you say that?" I asked.

"Until they told me I was leaving, I thought I'd be here forever. So, I inquired as to the possibility of returning one day, if even for a visit. That's when they informed me there may be nothing left to return to."

I was happy to have been sitting down.

She'd be gone in less than a month. She said she had some good-byes to do. I knew everybody loved her. This will be a difficult time for her. But just wait until Sunday at the service. And the visits we would make. But I looked forward to praying with her these next thirty days. It's the only thing that gives me hope. I really want to pray with her and for her.

But, what about me? What will I do without her? Why am I going to cry behind her back? I guess I'll be emotional on the day she leaves. But I'll have to pray until then. I need just as much preparation as she does. I just wonder what she'll do, where she'll go. I'm certain she has a plan. I pray she does or that she will. I know her better than that, though. She's a responsible person.

I sat down to lunch. She walked in and joined me at my table, our table. It has been for years. Her present behavior would suggest nothing has changed. She just sat down as usual and looked straight at me. I could hardly look at her. She had already served up more than her fair share of bad news for one day. What else could she possibly have to say to me now? I dreaded the answer to that question.

We ate in silence. I wasn't mad at her. And I didn't suppose she were angry toward me. But the awkwardness was thick as pea soup. It wasn't just that she was leaving but that I would soon be out of a job as well. I remembered, though, that she had spent the morning doing thing toward that end. Exactly, when was she leaving? Had the day of her departure been moved up? Was there a change in plans? Did she know a new thing? What was I in the dark about now? I was starting to get angry.

She must have sensed it because she began to speak.

"Is something wrong?"

"I don't know. You've dropped a couple of dingers on me today."

"I'm sorry. I just thought you wanted to know. I thought you deserved to know."

"Thank you for that."

I thought about what I just said. It may have come off a bit sarcastic.

"I'm sorry if I sound harsh," I said.

"No, you're not. I know what you meant. Besides, if anyone deserves to be angry, it's you. Because you're right, you've had a lot laid on you today."

"But, what can I do?"

Her demeanor changed to a sweet reassurance as she answered my question, "There's really nothing either of us can do. I'll move on. I'll pray for you and you'll pray for me. But for now...

She leaned forward and took my hand. "Let's pray together and finish the work at hand."

After lunch, we returned as one to the office we had shared for so many years. We both had plenty of work to do. I needed to go over my visitation list for Tuesday, look over my lesson for the Wednesday Bible story, prepare for Thursday's meeting, go over strategies for Saturday's outreach, and write Sunday's sermon. As you can see, I had plenty to occupy my mind. She had to prepare her music, her children's sermon, her Sunday School lesson, and her lesson for the women's meeting.

I prepared for Tuesday's visitation by preparing to be with her as she announced to everyone she was leaving. I wouldn't be easy. The kids would be especially disappointed. How would she explain it to them? They could never, and probably should never, about all the policy and procedure of mission work. All they knew was that they loved her.

I prayed for everyone on the list. The list generally consisted of one who missed Sunday services, a prospect, and one who might benefit from some upcoming event. It was difficult, really, for two people to visit more than that on any given Tuesday. Sometimes, though, we did manage a few more. But more often than not, that's all we got around to. They always seem to want to talk to and feed us. We just made a day of it and made no plans to return to the office.

I left work that evening kind of mellow and sad. I had things to do around my tiny apartment. So, I just planned a simple little evening with some soup and crackers, a little tv, and a lot of work. I even gave thought to updating my resume. But who would hire me at this stage in my life? I found some news on tv and relaxed in my chair. That's all my tiny apartment has is that chair and a love seat. I was lucky to have the love seat. Someone had at one time taken pity on me and donated it to my humble residence. I didn't pay rent anyway. It came to me as part of the salary package. I could eat in the cafeteria at work, live in that apartment, enjoy a small stipend twice a month and some pro bono medical care.

Dinner was just like I said it would be, soup and crackers. I had some old comedy shows I watched with dinner. There's a table in my kitchen but I always ate in front of the tv. I have been doing that since the passing of my dear wife a few years back. The tv is my only company. And noe they're taking away my best friend.

After dinner I went through some files. I wasn't even certain as to what it was I was searching for. I just needed to feel as though I had some sort of control of my own life. I thought I was doing pretty good up until today. I should've known it was all too good to last. But God knows best all the time. None of us can escape His wisdom. His will does and should prevail. But it all seems so unfair sometimes. What to do? What to do?

After finishing what I was doing, I sat down to some television. I didn't make it a habit of watching a lot of tv. I just didn't think it influenced me upward. All it spoke of was the woes of man. But for a few hours per night I would watch some old shows and the news. It relaxed me. The wife and I used to watch together, especially as she lay on her death bed.

After the news, I prepared to go to sleep. I had tried to sit through late night television before. But it was all full of gossip and idol worship. It seemed people who interviewed other people weren't at all interested in the lives of the interviewees as much as the interviewee seemed to be interested in advertising their new film or musical release. It was nothing but propaganda. And all the sex discussed was totally opposed to the commands of God. They seemed to brag about the ability to do as they pleased with whoever they pleased.

Well, I got ready for bed and prayed as I usually did. I read my Bible, sang an old hymn, and prayed. I thanked God for His love and mercy. I thanked Him for my best friend and colleague. I thanked Him for all the opportunities to work for Him and that He would work through me. I thanked Him for my good health.

But I had to confess a few things. I confessed my lack of trust in Him. I confessed my fears and anger about losing my partner. I confessed any negative influences I might have allowed in my life. I confessed any lustful and/or greedy thoughts and feelings at all. I was by no means a terribly abusive adulterer but I did have to admit to using feelings of loneliness to excuse lustful looks at coworkers and even on occasion parishioners. But mostly it was women on the street.

Next, I prayed for God's Spirit to work through the word at the mission. I prayed for my two offspring, who were everywhere. I prayed for family members on both mine and my late wife's side. I prayed for co-workers. I prayed especially for my partner. I prayed she would be the evangelist in this time both leaving here and going there. I prayed for traveling mercies granted to her as well.

I prayed for the people in our parish. I prayed for the lost. I prayed for the ones we had not seen in a while. I prayed for the regulars. And, finally, I prayed for the volunteers. I prayed for some friends who were struggling with different things. I prayed for our worship team as they prepared for Sunday. I prayed for those I had seen on the news last night. I find the news to be a good source for prayer fodder. And, finally, I prayed for all those women I looked at, not just saw.

The last part of my prayer was my surrender of everything beginning at my very relationship with God, His Son, His Spirit, and His word. I surrendered my continuous grief over my wife, and my loneliness for my children and family. But the surrender the impending loss of my coworker came as somewhat of a challenge. I just wasn't convinced I could do this without her. I still wondered why.

I found it easier, though, to surrender all those souls entrusted to me. I knew only God could do a ministry. He worked through me, so be it. I surrendered my health, my relationships, and my hobbies. But the surrender of lust came with conviction because I knew what He would have me do. After that, I read some more from my Bible and wrote it all down in a journal. But then I had to put feet to prayer.

We met in the office that morning. She looked like she was ready to cry. I knew she had a lot of reservations about this. She didn't want to say good-bye.

"I want to tell them why, but I know it wouldn't help," she started with.

"Let's just be careful what we tell them", I retorted.

"Yes, I know," she said, "but what if they ask?"

I couldn't reply to that. What could I say? After all, they will ask. What can she say? If she tells the truth, it could cause a few problems with the people. If she lies, she will not be able to stand herself.

"Should I lie?" she asked.

"I don't know."

I didn't know. I wasn't lying.

We got into the car and headed out. As usual, I drove. I knew exactly where I was going. I have to admit, though, I do have a few favorites among the people. She knew it as well. I think she also felt the same way. We pulled into the driveway of the first stop of our day. It belonged to a very nice, older lady. She was, I confess, my all-time favorite. She had accepted the gospel on the first try. She began at Sunday school and now teaches the same class.

She wanted to pray before we climbed out of the car. She cried.

She wept like Jesus wept. I held her hand. It felt like I was her father and we were going to see a neighbor after she broke one of her windows. But she had done nothing wrong. No, wrong had been done to her. It was all a beaurocratic error. But this woman would be very understanding no matter what the reason. She was a forgiving soul. But she also couldn't be lied to. You just didn't lie to people like her. So, we prayed. We thanked God for this one. She repented of her bad attitude. I prayed for her, she for I, and both for her.

We got out and walked up to the door. The door was promptly answered at my rap. She had seen us sitting outside. But somehow she perceived us as praying. And she did not wish to interrupt. But as now she gladly received our company. She answered in true appreciation of said company. She seemed in anticipation of a deeply spiritual visit. It seemed as though she would that we pray once again before entry but we all thought it time for a visit.

We proceeded inside and sat down. She offered food and I was hungry. But, what would I say? What could I say? Besides, we had some rather important news to share. I felt as though that were priority. But I still accepted cookies and milk as I was starving. And besides that, she had made said cookies in anticipation of our visit, as she usually had in the past. She expected us every Tuesday at this same time every week. As a matter of fact, we always made sure we did not arrive at lunchtime because we knew she would try to feed us. But it was always a nice visit and we never wanted to put her out. And she has always been very spirit-filled and in the word.

Well, during the conversation, we sensed a time to tell her. We looked at each other and prepared her.

I said, "Evelyn, we have something we want to tell you."

Then my partner interjected," Yes we do. I received some bad news yesterday."

Deep concern came over her counrenance. She sat straight up and said, "Oh, no, is something wrong?"

"No," my partner said, "nothing's wrong, per say. It's just that, well, they're letting me go."

"Letting you go?", Evelyn asked.

"Yes," she answered, "I'm going t have to go."

Go where?," Evelyn asked.

"I don't know."

Evelyn looked at me as though I might have some idea. I was still focused on my partner. It was like hearing the news all over again. But I still didn't believe it.

Evelyn asked me, "Have they said where she's going?"

The question stunned me.

"No," I answered nervously. I wished they would have.

We all said good-bye at the door. Evelyn had tears in her eyes. As did my partner.But not me.No, sir. I did not cry. I couldn't. I was still reeling over it. I also wondered as to what news I would hear next. I dared not ask the question as to what else could go wrong.

She wanted to go see a family next. They were a particular family whom she had been witness to seven births, although two were still-births. Only five remained. But they was still a big family. And they were very poor. I asked if she wanted to go get some supplies to take to them. But she seemed only desirous to visit with them.

We pulled up into the drive and were greeted by two dogs, one large and the other medium. They sniffed us. I may have feared them except I worried they were hungry. I wished we had brought supplies. They may starve by the time we return with food. I hoped the family might not have done so already.

Stage two of our welcome came in the form of two small boys. They were both the oldest and second youngest of the children. There was one other boy, but, as it turned out, he wasn't felling as well as these two. The second oldest child, a girl, was more than likely sitting with him. He was the baby, after all. The other girl was a bit of a loner.

As they were familiar with us, we were greeted as friends. They also corralled the dogs who, by the way, were neither mean or angry in any way. But they didn't want them to run off. It was their job to corral them. And that they did as they informed us their dad was working with their uncle and mom was busy inside. My heart went out to these boys. They loved their parents.

We sat down in the living area. It was kind of messy, but bearable. I always thought highly of Alice as a home maker. She always does the best she can considering she's got kids afoot. And John wasn't a great help. But he tried his best to stay out of the way. And he did a fair job of keeping the kids out of the way as well. They really were a nice family.

"How's things?", I asked the couple.

Alice answered before John could, "Kids are alright. Couple of 'em got colds."

Then it was John's turn, "Yeah, they got 'em at school."

I answered, "I'm sure they'll be all right."

The tension between us was beginning to be felt by all. It was like they knew we had purpose for presence. They knew something had to be going on. Yes, we had visited before but somehow this visit was different. We felt it too, knowing we came here to inform this nice family that one of their favorite people in the whole world was to depart company soon. But the questions here were how and when. And there was the question of whom as well.

"Um, look."

She looked at the couple.

"I'm, uh, I'm leaving…here…soon."

Alice dried her hands as she walked toward us. She said, "Where you going?"

He kind of looked at us as well as if to ask the same question.

She answered, "I'm just going away."

Alice inquisoned, "Why?"

My partner drew a breath.

"The powers that be have decided…"

That's what went through her head to say. I knew this because she would tell me later.

But, instead, she said, "It's just time for me to go."

I felt like I had to step up next to her on this one.

So, I said, "I have to agree. It's hard to say good-bye but it's just time.

There was a lot of hugging and crying up to the time we left. The children were brought in to say good-bye as well. Some thought I was leaving as well but we reassured them that I was going nowhere.

We finished all of our visits and good-byes. People just couldn't accept that se was going away. Some were angry, some at her, some at me, others at the organization. I completely understood that one. I too harbored resentment toward the organization. None of this seemed fair. They were ridding me of my partner, my friend (Carol, by the way). What would I do without her?

Carol appeared tired and worn out. I kind of felt like one more day on the job might be her undoing. Maybe she needed to go, to get some rest. This job of ours was not an easy one, indeed. We performed services on Sundays and support groups on Sunday and Wednesday nights. We also did sundry ministry such as food pantry and clothes closet on Mondays and Thursdays. On Tuesdays, we visited shut-ins and families on Fridays. But we rested on Saturday.

Just thinking about it all made me tired. Maybe I'll go with her. We always made a good team. No, I'd better stay here. But all that sounds like a lot of work for one man. I'll do it leisurely. What doesn't get done just won't get done. The organization will just have to accept that. I just didn't care anymore even if it meant my job.

"Aren't you going to say it?" she asked.

My thought pattern had been interrupted.

"Say what?" I asked.

"Good-bye. I'm leaving, remember?"

"No, I'm not saying it, not yet."

"Then, when?"

"Before you go, I promise. Besides, I haven't got your going away gift yet."

"Oh, don't bother. Besides, the church should do that."

"No, I'll do something. I'm sure they expect it from me."

"You always do what's expected, don't you?"

"I must. It's the way it has to be."

"Says who?"

I couldn't come up with an answer for that. She remained quiet the rest of the way back. She still had two weeks until her final good-byes from this place. It was two weeks until her final good-bye speech at the mission church. That's all the time I had left.

The next two weeks just seemed to fly by. The next thing I knew we were up to her final service. I did buy her a parting gift. The church raised the money and I, of course, volunteered to purchase the gift. She had offered again and again to buy me a gift. But I felt that she was to be the recipient of the only gift that was to be purchased on this occasion. After, she was in the ejector seat.

I went to see if she had her good-bye speech ready. I wanted to be sure it was acceptable and appropriate. I don't know why I was suddenly so concerned about her speech writing. She certainly possesses more eloquence than I. She usually proof-reads my work before I present a sermon. No, I was just going to say good-bye. I just need to deal with my emotions.

2

Everyone filed in and filled in the seats at the mission. As he approached the podium, he could see everyone there. He saw all the people they had visited the week before. But also he noticed a few he hadn't seen in a while. All were here to say good-bye to a wonderful friend. But, wait, that sounds like they're all in attendance at her funeral as opposed to a simple farewell gathering. He did, however, sort of feel like he was saying a final farewell.

He approached the microphone and began to speak.

"Ladies and gentlemen, I'm sure you know why we're all here. I thank you all for coming out today. As most of you know, the Missions Committee in all of its wisdom, has decided to downsize the organization by one very special missionary. But, all of that aside, we've come to express our love and appreciation to Carol."

He read Isaiah 61:1 about the prisoners, the poor and needy, the widows, orphans and others who needed ministering to. Afterward, Carol led everyone in a couple of songs. Then a volunteer prayed, followed by a special song performed by the children's choir. Carol had been working with them on some music, her swan song. Today, they would give it back. This was work that she truly loved. She loved the music and the kids.

It was then his time to deliver the message. He had to hold back his resentment. He resented not only the committee for firing her but also her for not being bitter about it. He had to pray, hard, right now for strength, for wisdom, for a calm spirit. He confessed a lack of forgiveness toward the committee members. He prayed for Carol and for all of those here.

Then he spoke:

"This morning, I am reading from the book of Isaiah. This particular scripture means so much to me because it speaks directly to me as a servant of God. But it also speaks to others in ministry as well. I think of Carol when I read this. All those mentioned in it are all of those Carol has touched in her ministry here. She's dedicated to this.

"I will carry on alone. But, what indeed can one lone missionary hope to possibly accomplish? Do you know the worst part? I can't sing.

He thought he heard an amen.

"Anyway, my wife and I started in this mission fifteen years ago. I knew from day one it was meant to be. But neither of us could sing.

He didn't give someone the opportunity to amen this time.

"We had no sense of music at all He looked, but nothing from those who would oh too quickly agree he had no musical inclination.

"But five years after our arrival, Carol brought in a myriad of talents, including music."

His sermon went on to evangelize the lost, bring the wanderers back to the fold, and to challenge mission volunteers to carry on the work of a genius. He couldn't say enough good things about her. His voice began to soften as he felt her warmth, her friendship, her support. What would he do without her to hold him up? He felt as though he had wandered after that before.

He announced,

"There will be a reception in the meeting hall."

He still felt resentful but he felt something else as well. It was an old, familiar feeling. He felt like he was losing someone just like before. Or, was it just a familiar loss?

Everyone gathered in the meeting hall. Some had left already.

Still, a few other had straggled in who had not been present at the service. But, mostly, it was all who had stayed after. She had been approached in the hall by a few of them. She talked in the hallway, something she has always done. People seemed to enjoy her company to a few extreme levels of preoccupation. She had been just thet popular.

But he had never appreciated it. He wanted her to be where he wanted her when he wanted to see her there. What was his hurry, though? He made his way into the hall to inspect everything. He sought assure things were just as he requested. He guessed she had it just the way she wanted it, talking to everyone who desired her company. So, he would be patient.

Finally, she made it inside. He approached the makeshift podium and promptly requested everyone's attention. She took the hint as well as her seat behind him. Also, a member of the Association sat there beside her along with a few other important people in the community. Then, someone walked in through the hallway door. Carol stood and went out to greet her. It was Carol's niece. He had met her once before.

After the two of them took their seats, he continued to speak.

"Ladies and Gentlemen", he began, "I want to thank you all for coming. This will be our last chance to say farewell to our friend and companion, Carol. So, without further adieu, a few words from Carol. Carol?"

She approached the microphone. He almost hugged her but refrained instead. She just smiled stood at the mic.

"My precious friends", she began, "I stand before you a mere servant of God. That's really all that I've done for the past ten years. I have been richly blessed. And it's been a privilege to know each of you."

She continued to speak but he wasn't hearing what he wanted to hear. He wanted to hear bitterness, resentment, betrayal. But, instead, all he heard was a whole lot about the will of God. He just couldn't stand to think of this as the actual will of God. How could it be God's will to take her out of here where she has done so much for Him?

No, it couldn't be. It had to be that the Association was in disobedience to God. They probably voted not to obey Him. It had to be God's will for her to remain here. But beaurocratsare just that way, even in ministry.With the Association, it's all about the bottom line, the almighty dollar. They chose in this circumstance to obey their idol. They chose to obey money over God. That was his feeling, anyway.

Then, all of a sudden, all eyes were on him. Her speech was done. They all looked to him for direction. What now?

He stood and returned to the mic.

"Now, we present Carol with a token of our affection."

The Association member present looked on with apparent eagerness. But he wouldn't be so happy after he saw that what was bought for her wasn't on their list of potential parting gifts.

Our missionary reached down and picked up a guitar case. It wasn't empty.

"Carol, when you first came to us, we had no music. We did our very best, but neither my wife or I could carry a tune.

He guessed the person from before had left already, figures.

So, today we give back to you one of the many things you have given to us. We present you with this guitar."

She cried as she approached him and accepted his very thoughtful gift. Her niece cried as well. Everyone cheered. This time he let her hug him. But it was cold and just about unfeeling from his end. He would cry later, alone.

She spent the evening with her niece. He let the volunteers run the 12-step group. He was at the mission but he didn't feel like he was. He was in an old, familiar place. He'd been here before but not in a literal sense. He was in his mind. But he felt like he was going out of it. He just couldn't accept this as the will of God. And he really couldn't stand the fact that Carol thought it was. He just couldn't reconcile that.

As he spent time in prayer that evening, he gave his feelings to God. That's when he realized that Carol was not only not angry at them, she was also not angry with him. As a matter of fact, she wasn't angry about anything. But, then again, her still, quiet spirit was just her way. So, what's the matter with him?

He didn't get a lot of sleep. He felt abandoned and suddenly very alone. But this feeling seemed to extend way past merely her. This ran soul deep. Watch tv, go for a walk, pray some more... it was the only way. When he finally did sleep, he dreamed of an empty mission. He heard music in his dream but nobody was playing it. Nobody was there at all. He wasn't even certain of his own presence.

He had no motivation to come to work on Monday. He didn't know if he could make it all the way there, even if he did live close by. It still seemed miles away. But, what else could he do today? Where else would he go? If he didn't go in today, when would he? Why did he ask these questions? He never did before, or did he? Who would answer them anyway?

He did go to work. He happened to notice the lack of change in the atmosphere. Were they going forward without her? He didn't know if he could do it. He walked into the mission and saw her packing her office. Her niece was lending a hand. Would he want to help out? No, there's no way. It seemed terribly self-defeating to help her leave him. If anything, he would unpack those boxes. No, he just wanted to go to his own office and not leave until 5:00.

But at eleven, he got a visitor, Carol.

"Ready for lunch?" she asked in a mood not befitting such betrayal.

"Lunch, ...sure."

He got up and accompanied her to the lunchroom.

There was never any charge to anyone in this lunchroom. It received its support from the Association. It was run by volunteers in what was known as the Kitchen Committee. There existed several such committees. There was one for every area of ministry. It had been Carol's responsibility to oversee and coordinate all volunteer activities. And, so, as they traversed the serving line, everyone knew her. Some even knew she was leaving.

The silence was deafening as they sat and gave thanks. She broke it.

"Well, you still haven't said it."

"Said what?"

"Good-bye?"

"Uh, what about yesterday?"

"Yesterday, everybody came here to see me off. They all said their good-byes. But, you haven't said it yet."

"I guess I was going to."

"When?"

"I don't know."

"Why don't you help me by using your car to haul my boxes to my house? Then you can say it."

"I could do that."

They finished lunch in a more relaxed mood. But he was beginning to feel sad. Reality was setting in hard as he began to see her go away. He really was about to say good-bye, like before. And afterward, the long drive back.

He thought to himself, Just finish your food and get to it.

He drove her home. Her niece was there packing some dishes and a few other items. They arrived and got out of the car. He made his way around to the back seat and…slowly began to lug her boxes out of the car and to her house, the house. It would no longer be her home. She went into the house to check her niece's progress. He carried a box inside. Still, there were others to be brought inside as well. He stood just inside the door, box in hand. They saw him as he came in.

Carol pointed and spoke, "Take that one over there."

He did as directed and set it down slow. He'd been here before but it wasn't all packed up.

"Thanks," she said as she slowly stood back up.

Then they went out.

Each carried in a box from the car. He spotted a trailer hitched to the niece's SUV. That trailer would carry her things into the wild blue yonder and take her away forever. They each carried their respective boxes into the house. They placed them into the exact spot that Carol wished to load them from on the next fateful day. They had to be loaded just right. But he needed to get back to work sometime today. And she realized that, so…

"Well, that's that", she said.

"Yeah", he answered, "that's all of them."

She walked outside behind him and hugged him in front of the whole world. He cried, but not a lot so the whole world could see.

"Good-bye, Carol. I'll miss you."

He left.

A whole era stood in his rear-view mirror. He would have to pull the car over if these tears continued. Seeing through them proved difficult at best. As was saying good-bye. But it did prove impossible. Indeed he old miss her but he would somehow go on. He had already decided that without her that what got done would get done but what didn't, well, it just wouldn't.

He arrived back at the now lonely mission and went straight to his cave, his office. He sat behind his desk and felt a sense of relief it was over. She really was gone from him. This he'd felt before, the anticipation, the departure, and finally the good-byes. He'd said good-bye before. And it had been a lot more dramatic the first time. But this time he was counting his losses *and* licking his wounds.

But soon he was visited. Not by her this time but by a volunteer at his door.

"Excuse me, sir", he began.

He was a volunteer from a local church serving on the decorating committee.

"Everything alright?" Al inquired.

"No, sir, we have a problem."

Of course.

The man continued, "We're decorating the hall but there are too many of us."

Al looked at him for more detail.

So, he continued, "Sir, we have ten volunteers in the hall. We only really need five of us. Otherwise, we're falling all over each other. But nobody wants to leave."

In what universe is having too many volunteers a problem? He almost stood up to go and handle the situation personally but remained seated instead.

"Uh, your name?" Al asked the volunteer.

"Bob, sir."

"Bob, here's what I want you to do. Go back there and pick out four people to work with. Start at one end of the hallway and work toward the middle. If the other five have not finished their end of the hallway, just finish the job. Okay?"

Bob nodded and ran off.

No need to get up on this one.

Later in the afternoon, Al went for a walk around the mission. He wanted to get a picture in his head of current operation status. He as starting to realize just what carol did around there. She was the coordinator of the volunteers, one of many hats she wore. She also served as worship leader, choir director, teacher, secretary, and a few others. Just what did *he* do around there? He wasn't certain if he did anything at all.

But he also thought about the fact that she had been an administrator but not much of a delegator. She could manufacture a schedule but she couldn't delegate authority. She was forever afraid she'd hurt somebody's feelings if she chose another over them. That's the very thing he feared he'd run into now.

He went first to the kitchen to check on things in there. It was kind of messy but passable. The Health Department didn't come around much. That was because there was no charge for the meals.

They only concerned themselves when tax money was involved. If it were a for profit restaurant, it would be different. But as it is, they only complained if the freezer didn't freeze, the refrigerator didn't fridgerate, moldy food, bugs, etc... But they had none of those problems, he hoped.

He walked around the kitchen, greeting as he inspected. A few asked about Carol. He said that he'd seen her off. He looked around before finally spotting the schedule she had put together. It was a work of administrative art. She truly was a master with the office software utilized at the center. It was a nice little table with rows and columns. On it were names, days, times, and responsibilities.

But there was a blank line on top of the table. The line was labeled "Crew Chief". No one was appointed to be in charge. He caught himself before inquiring as to who was in charge. He knew better than to ask that question in a room full of volunteers. Either all would step up or no one would. They had no idea who was in charge. Oh, each indeed did have an idea but it was the wrong one. If they knew what each other was thinking, they'd be at each other's throats.

Then a noise interrupted his thoughts. It was yelling from down the hall. He didn't recognize the voice. But whoever it was seemed really upset. He heard what sounded like maybe cussing as well as a few threats. What was going on down there? He remembered the conversation with Bob earlier. He wondered if that had anything to do with it. So, he followed the sound...

He arrived at the source of the yelling. There he found an older gentleman yelling at the man from before. Bob didn't seem to be yelling back. But it did appear as though he were attempting to speak. The other gentleman was throwing his hands around while he said things about not being treated like a slave, that he was a grown man, something about how he should be in charge. Al spoke up...

"What's the problem, gentlemen?"

The other guy answered first.

"He came in here barking orders about these four people

(pointing) being on his crew and the rest of us working at the end of the hall."

"Yeah," Al answered, "that's what I told him."

"Who are you?"

"Al Bryant, Director of the mission."

"Al, I've served on this committee since Carol first started. Therefore, I should be in charge if anybody."

"Then, why didn't *you* come to my office and ask for direction like he did?"

"'Cause I ain't no rat."

"Bob stepped up and took responsibility, so he's in charge."

"I'm done."

He walked out.

Al told Bob to finish the hall. He thanked all of them. He really did appreciate his volunteers. Now, he began to understand Carol's feelings about them.

As he drove home, he realized she hadn't actually left yet. She wouldn't be leaving until early tomorrow. But he'd already said good-bye. So, officially, she was gone. This was crazy. He missed her and she wasn't even gone, not yet. What about when she does leave tomorrow? Is that a different kind of missing someone, when they're actually gone? But, is it her that he missed? It felt like there was more involved.

That evening he found he could still pray for her before she left. He did. He prayed for her safety and for her to find a way to make a living. He lifted up her niece. He went on to ask God to help him make sense of all of this.

"God," he prayed, "how can such a thing be in Your will?"

No answer.

Tuesday arrived and he didn't know how to do the visits alone. Where would he go? Who would he see? Should he go at all? How would this play out? She just left and he was really finding out how much he needed her. Visiting single women and widows was certainly out of the question. What about visiting kids? *She* was always good at that. And, what would he say when and if they asked…about…her?

Then he remembered he'd not made his periodic visit to the retirement village. He usually made that visit about every three weeks to a month. Carol hadn't always gone with him on these visits. He didn't actually require her on this one. He just went room to room visiting residents, nurses, workers, family, friends, and others who frequented this place. And he was always blessed at this place.

As usual, he began in the room of Ms. Ester Sims, 90 years old. Her 62 year old son-in-law was estranged to her. Years ago, they had a big falling-out. There was no peace there. Her daughter came to see her once a week, without him. It grieved her that he wouldn't come with her. Al provided as much comfort to the both of them as he could muster. It was a sad situation indeed. And he felt useful, even without her. But, just how useful was he?

He returned to his office feeling refreshed and regenerated. As a matter of fact, he stopped on the way at a drive-in burger joint. He pulled his car up and just sat there at first. He smiled at the thought of just how much good he had done today, all by himself. Yep, that settled it, that would be his Tuesday visitation stop from here on out. The problem, though, was deciding which he'd do first, the home or the drive-thru.

He ordered one of those double bags meant for two. But he was hungry enough to devour both by himself. It came with two drinks. He had to personally request ketchup because, for some reason, they did not automatically supply that with the meal. He didn't mind, though. He felt liberated. He learned real fast that he could do ministry all by himself. So, he ate with the most abundant joy he could muster.

What other ministries could he do by himself? He could both

write and deliver sermons by himself. He never really needed her for that. He'd given up running those by her a long time ago. She just couldn't seem to handle his…honesty. She was too apologetic. He never apologized. But, maybe that was a problem.

He went back to the office, the empty office. Now it was all very real again. She had just left that very day and his emotions were already on a roller coaster. He was down that morning, up in the afternoon, and now down again. What exactly was he driven by? He sat for a minute to take some notes on his visit. He would need these to fill out his periodic reports. But, he was terribly distracted.

He went home that evening but he didn't stay there. He went out to be with some people. They weren't religious people, although a few of them have been known to darken the doors of the mission church once or twice. One of them attended completely by accidence once. He apologized profusely but Al reassured him there was no need. It appeared he had meant to go somewhere else, but along the way…

He had a good time in spite of himself. He had intended to. He put everything out of his head as he had done many times before. He made up his mind to do something for himself a couple of days a week. Yeah, he would apply himself a couple of days a week. But Tuesday and Friday would belong to him. It was apparent the Association didn't care if anything got accomplished, not anymore. They had pretty much signed over to him his license to kill (not literally).

He watched television for several hours that evening. He even watched shows he always thought were bad for him. His body began to wear down. He was tired and sore. Why was he sore? What had he done? He turned fifty. That's what he did. That removed the mystery of his soreness, his aging body. Fifty wasn't old but it wasn't young either.

He slept well, with a little guilt. He dreamed about the home. In his dream, he felt inadequate. He just couldn't seem to get anything accomplished. In his dream, he tried to walk down a hallway to take some food to someone but the hallway just kept getting longer. He never made it there. He just got tired and dropped the food. He began to shake uncontrollably. He fell to his knees.

The next morning was Wednesday. He knew what he had to do. He had to get on his knees in the chapel and beg God's forgiveness. He had let himself go. He had given up on God. He had given up on his calling. He had given up on himself. What would Carol say to him right now? Oh, yeah, that wound, and one much deeper.

He decided once he arrived at work to go straight to his office. It would only take a minute. He just felt like he needed to check in. Why did he all of a sudden feel like acting responsibly? Wasn't he mad at *them?* Yes, but he would not allow them to change him. He was still a sure-footed man of God. Okay, do your job today. Today is a day of teaching, literally. There was a class he taught on Wednesday.

Today, he taught the gospel of Christ to a group of people. He taught about getting saved. It was first and foremost. He believed that nothing in life began before you were born again. He felt like life began with new life in Christ. You're just dead before that. And he taught the concepts of this every Wednesday. But, first things first.

He prayed after lunch for all who would attend. Used to join him in this prayer. But he was a lone wolf now. Better said, he was a lone missionary. He would have to pray about that particular situation. Today, he would feel that really strong because here he felt like he was doing the work of a missionary. Spreading the gospel was at the heart of mission work. It was the cornerstone of his work.

His class piled into the chapel. A few seemed to be searching around the room for something, or someone. One person even asked.

"She left yesterday," he answered matter-of-factly.

"Where did she go?"

"I don't know."

"Is she coming back?"

"No."

That answer turned the questioner away. He felt as though he needed to make an announcement. So, he announced, once everyone had sat down, that Carol had resigned. He informed them of why, exactly. Some said they already knew. A few others were actually surprised. And still others didn't believe it.

This class he taught was an evangelism class. He wasn't, however, teaching them how to evangelize. He would teach that at a later date. No, in this class, he taught people how to get saved. That's right. He preached and taught them from the gospels, the book of Romans, and a few of the epistles. Some said it was works salvation, but it wasn't.

No, he wanted them to know what they were getting into. He wasn't into the numbers game. He wasn't trying to save thousands so as to impress others. He taught them what it was to repent. He taught them about sin and confession. He taught them that Jesus forgave sin if we confessed it. Some said it was a class to impress upon others how to *earn* their salvation. Still others claimed he taught a form of legalism.

On his reports to the Association, they continually asked him how many people he shared the gospel with. He believed that if he shared the gospel with only one person, he was adding to the kingdom. Angels would rejoice. But the Association would certainly reject that as an acceptable use of his resources, which they provided. They would cut off his funding.

But he considered this a good compromise. He though that if he could bring people to this class, that would be an acceptable number to write on the report. He also knew that if he told people he was gonna share the gospel, they wouldn't attend. But they would certainly attend a Bible study. Bible studies are usually so generic. People come because it's like going to church on Wednesday night. They've done that for years.

Some of these people have participated in what he termed "Service

Projects". They would all go out and serve in the community doing things like handy work, grass mowing, baby-sitting, trash hauling, etc... His kitchen did a shut-in ministry taking meals around to those who couldn't leave their homes for one reason or another.

In the summer, he encouraged (even challenged) his congregation to be witnesses for Christ. After all, that was the crust of mission work. His vision was to start an actual church. As it was, church was held at the mission. He didn't actually attend church anywhere. He didn't have time. He was kept busy by the work at the mission. He figured that's where his church would come out of, but not right now.

A revival was held every fall. They also hosted a harvest party. The Association he do more for Halloween. But he didn't believe in Halloween. He knew it had become a satanic holiday over the years. Human sacrifices were rumored. He didn't know if he believed those rumors but t was just the reason for the rumors.

The harvest party kicked off the holidays as far as he was concerned. He began to decorate early, like in October, for All Saints Day, Thanksgiving, Christmas, and New Years. Folks though him a bit eccentric. But he knew what he believed in. And he supported it at all times. The Association had asked him over and over again to throw a Halloween party for kids but he didn't feel like represented the mission well.

Speaking of the Association and report writing, Thursday morning would find him in his office filling those out as best he could or as much as he felt like. He was troubled by the wording, the lack of 'missionness'. They did not appear interested at all in the spread of the gospel message quite as much as justification for the expenditures passed forward, having to give more money.

As he tried to write, the phone succeeded in ringing.

He answered as etiquette would demand, "Hello, this is Al Bryant."

It was someone from the Association.

"Al, Fred here, how's things there?"

"Oh, fine, I was just..."

"Don't mean to interrupt your work there, Al. Just wanted to talk a little about the Southern Association Sports League."

They always tried to get him to get people from his association involved in the recreation department of other associations. They had not any sports in their association. Some issues in the past had sprung up over those things.

How did they expect him to get those reports done if they kept calling him whenever he was trying to fill them out? Maybe he would just not do the reports and whenever they inquired as to the reason, he'd inform them it was because they kept calling whenever he tried to fill them out.

His thoughts were interrupted by the man on the other end.

"Well, what are you gonna do?"

"I'm gonna do what I always do."

"What's that, nothing?"

"No, I'll announce it at service on Sunday."

"Promotion, Al, promotion is the key to success."

Al thought attraction was the key here.

3

He always felt like people should see what the mission does in the community and want to be a part of it. He wanted them to approach him with the question of why they do what they do. His desire was for people to see something here and want it. He wanted them to see the hope that was in him. They always saw it in Carol. If only he could exemplify that same sense of hope, that same enthusiasm she did. If only he could believe as she did.

The caller had said his good-bye and hung up the phone on his end. What had been the point of it? What was the point of these reports? Was there any point? He doubted it. He just sat and stared at the report sitting unfinished in front of him. Why had someone created this report with these questions, these blanks to fill in? He bore down on it with all the concentration he could muster.

But time snuck up on him. Before he knew it, lunch time was upon him. Oh, well, I guess it'll have to wait an hour. He wondered how he could ignore this any longer. Fill out the report, answer the questions. Fill in the blanks. Then, send it in to someone who will probably just set it aside for future use. What if you forget to sign them? Then at least they can't hold you accountable to how you answered the questions and filled in the blanks. How many did you preach the gospel to? How many conversions? They're just keeping score.

After lunch, he got right back to it. He managed to finish, but it was sloppy. He had applied little to no effort to it. If they got sent back, so be it. He sent them out and went about his walk of the place. He looked around. He checked on the volunteers. Some were decorating for an upcoming banquet. Also, people were arriving from the surrounding area, seeking different types of service.

He provided assistance to all that he could possibly help. He prayed for the others. He handed out clothing and food, some advice as well. Once again, he was feeling the loss. She had helped a lot. He felt like he had done all that he could. But it was only half done. And he did it without help, without hope. He just went through the motions. It wasn't that he didn't feel anything. He just had so much going on in his head right now that he couldn't stop to think about it.

His day had come to an end so he went home. He prepared a meal and relaxed with his thoughts. He ended up watching tv that evening. He was doing more of that recently than he had done in the past. It just proved to be a relaxing activity. It required nothing of him. But it provided a lot of entertainment. Some of the things he saw on it, though, were a tad worldly in nature.

He went to bed with thoughts of report filing and volunteers, deadlines and recreational activity. He kept thinking about all the empty holes Carol left for him to fill and all the roles she played that simply left alongside her. He couldn't fill those shoes if he tried. He made no plans to attempt it. He would simply fulfill his own obligations. He would do his job and no other. It was their fault. If they didn't like it, they could send someone else to do it or come to do it themselves. They shouldn't have sent her away.

His weekend was restless. He could hardly sleep on Thursday evening. He dreamed all night about reports and phone calls. He dreamt of the struggle with coordination of the volunteers, delegating lay leadership, and handing out food and clothes. In his dream, he was worn down till he could hardly move. He looked around but found no help from anyone.

He was so tired on Friday, he stopped for coffee. He pulled into the parking lot of the mission and just sat in his car, staring at the building. It was an empty building without her, he thought. Without whom? Was there another presence here to haunt him? He dared not breach the outer perimeter of the building. He must prepare today to do work he doesn't feel like doing. He must oppose himself on this one.

If there ever were a lazy day, this was it. He didn't feel like doing anything, with the possible exception of absolutely nothing. Was that doing anything, doing nothing? Exactly where should he do nothing? Should he go into his office and do nothing? After all, nobody watched over him. He had no immediate supervision. The Association watched from afar. But there were, however, people around there who seemed to be their eyes.

How else would they keep hearing rumors of things going on there? Somebody must be watching from the inside and reporting. There were pastors who attended all Association functions, hob-knobbed with the higher-ups. And, sometimes, he spotted one or two hanging around. Were they spies? Or, were they concerned members of the Ministerial Alliance? Were they concerned or merely nosey?

He took the trek from car to office. It was a lonely walk, knowing Carol would not be waiting inside for him. But there was someone else who wouldn't be there, or anywhere, ever again. He approached the door leading inside ever so slowly. What was stopping him from turning around and not coming back to work? After all, it was Friday.

He made it to the door and proceeded indoors. People milled around. Some were the members of the Ministerial Alliance so alluded to earlier. Volunteers wandered about. Some asked of Carol. Did they not know? Of course they didn't know. She had only been gone a week. So, of course, some had not received the news yet. How long would he be answering these questions, having to relive that heartache over again and again. How long would it take them to acknowledge and accept the reality of her goneness?

It felt weird in his office. He didn't want to do the work because the people he worked for didn't want to help him get the job done. As a matter of fact, they hindered his job, the gospel, by removing his help, his right arm. They amputated him. Maybe there was something else he could be doing today. But he would have to do it, whatever it was, here at the office. He never knew who was watching, reporting, both, either.

He sat at his desk and intended to do nothing. He could perform that function very easily from his chair. But, until lunch? Maybe, he could read. What if somebody walked by, or worse, in, and saw him reading? That was the worst thing that could happen. What if word made its way back to the Association that he was spotted reading on their time? Were they paying him to read? No, they were not.

He was right. Somebody did come by. They even came in. This young man had long hair antye-dye. He still wore his sunglasses, even in the building. He was carrying a guitar, not in its case. He looked so young and yet so old. He had that old hippie look. Was he a forty year-old teenager? If he was as cool as he appeared, he probably was not a concerned member of the MA.

"Excuse me, sir," he began.

"Yes, can I help you? Al replied.

He seemed so polite, more polite than Al would have guessed him to be.

"Young man, is there something I can do for you?"

"Uh, where's Carol?"

"She's gone."

His face froze. His jaw dropped. His eyes became misty. Al realized what he said and how it was heard.

So, he explained, "No, no. She's not dead. She resigned."

Now, he was confused, of course.

"Resigned, sir? Why? She never said anything about…quitting."

Al realized he still didn't know who this guy was.

He stuck out his hand, "Al Bryant, Director. And, you are?"

"Boyd, Clay Boyd. I'm a musician."

He held up his guitar.

Then, he continued, "We had been talking about me playing here sometime, perhaps at a service."

"You're a musician?"

"Yes, I usually play clubs and bars, professional venues you understand? But, she had talked about my playing at church, like, for money."

They had never paid a musician before. He certainly wasn't starting now. Most were volunteers from churches. Paying this young fellow certainly was not a consideration.

They sat in the office and talked about Carol and why she resigned. Clay put to voice what Al's feelings had been when the Association, in all their infinite wisdom, decided to downsize her. His outspoken reaction matched Al's inner turmoil. But, still, he asked about playing and getting paid. Upon rejection for the paid gig, he insisted upon payment for all of his troubles of inquiry. He seemed to indicate there may have been a breach of contract. Al did not agree that there existed any necessity for compensation, financial or otherwise.

Clay left in a huff. Clearly, he had come in today just to get money. Had Al offered him money for nothing, he probably would've taken it. He had dealt with a lot of people in his day. Clay wasn't the hardest of characters he had had dealings with. That reminded him, though, that he was due to visit the prison again soon. A DOM didn't start churches. He maintained them. But Clay would probably not return. There was no money to be had.

What had Carol done here? He knew she was soft-hearted, an easy mark. That was kind of a good thing for him, though, because there had been a few instances where he had deserved a swift kick and she hadn't administered it. But, now people seemed to expect him to also be a soft touch as well. They were going to find out the hard way, though, he was an entirely different animal. He gave out no charity here. There did exist the possible exceptions, the widows, the orphans, the poor, but not any greedy musicians. Breach of contract, did he say? There existed no such agreement for payment with this young fellow.

Lunch time! He was going out. Maybe he wouldn't return today, or ever. No, he will return sometime, maybe not today, but sometime. It was a small town but there was a bigger one close by. This he did from time to time. He had his favorite haunts. And the drive to and fro was relaxing. What to order, though, and where to go to order?

He opted for the usual burger and fries. He had, invariably, become a creature of habit. Besides, he preferred eating around familiar faces. He had friends who ate there and all the waitresses knew him. He went in and sat down. The wait was just as usual as well. He did, however, feel strange about walking around alone. It seemed as though all eyes were on him. Maybe he heard some whispers going on around him. Had he dropped her off somewhere on the way? Is something wrong? Where is she?

"The usual, today, Al?" Queried the waitress.

He came out of his thoughts just long enough to reply.

"Uh, yeah, please. Thank you."

It was nice to be remembered.

She wrote it down and walked away.

He felt abandoned again.

She returned with his usual Root Beer, half ice.

"All alone, today, Al?" she asked with partial concern.

"Uh, yes, 'fraid so."

"Okay, just asking."

She didn't even seem to care. What was wrong with these people? Didn't they even notice?

He felt kind of out of place as he sat and ate his big burger with everything on it. Ketchup was on the table and he used a lot of it. It just wasn't the same. As a matter of fact, it was weird that he ate alone. He knew Carol wouldn't be with him and he still sat by himself. There were others there he was aquainted with. Why hasn't he sat with them?

So, after he ate and paid, He strolled over to one of them. Of course, the first question would be the same question asked by the waitress. Was he alone? He certainly was alone, probably for the remainder of his life. But he wasn't alone entirely. He had friends right there. And they asked if he would be at the bowling alley that evening. You better believe he will be there. He was cutting himself loose from all the bonds he'd attached himself to. He was going to enjoy himself tonight.

He'd gone every Friday night for a few years now. But, tonight he'd come for acceptance and acknowledgement. He needed to feel wanted, almost to the point of seeing his own face on a 'wanted' poster. Maybe there's a milk carton somewhere with his face on it. Boy, was he feeling lonely! To be in need of the company of these friends of his was a bad sign. He loved them like brothers, but why all of a sudden does he require their company?

He talked and he laughed the whole time he was there. It was as though he had it in him the whole time. Carol would approve and he knew it. He neither laughed or talked about anything immoral, anything that would compromise his position. He almost felt, however, like he had no control of his own emotions tonight. He expressed things, laughed them off as silly jargon, and moved on to other things. He didn't know what he would say or do next.

He arrived at home that evening, *really*tired. It would prove to be a dreamless night of sleep. The crickets chirped. They'd done that before. He walked in and readied for a great night of sleep. But since it was not a work night, he would stay up with a cup of hot coco. He read a little from a book he hadn't finished. He has always suffered interruptions whenever he tried to read.

He awoke in his reading chair. It had been a while since that happened. He felt as though he were in a dream as he wandered off to his room for sleep. He also had not changed clothes yet. Tomorrow was Saturday. He could change his clothes then. Tonight, he would just plop down on the bed. But the bed was empty. Who had been there before? He seemed suddenly lonely. Then he remembered a time many years ago he had fallen asleep in his chair and come to bed late on a Friday.

He began to get ready for bed, be he could not concentrate on what he was doing. It was the same routine every night. But for some reason, he couldn't think of what he was doing. Just looking at the bed confused him. There seemed to be something, or somebody missing from it. He kind of felt as though he had traveled back in time. Nothing seemed normal.

He turned away from the bedroom and wandered toward where he always thought the bathroom was. He felt dizzy but he thought he was just tired. He found himself in a groove he couldn't explain. He looked around a house he didn't recognize. He thought he'd gone back in time. If he had, then something or somebody was missing. It was then that he managed to find the bathroom. It looked like a long hallway.

He walked into the bathroom and made the immediate left turn at the sink. Then he looked head-long into the mirror. It was him, back to reality. Who was this man in his mirror? He didn't even know for sure. At one time he did. At one time, years ago, he knew exactly who this man was. He asked God the question that lingered in his head.

Pretty soon, he was actually ready for bed. Somehow, he managed to get ready. Falling asleep required no effort. He had felt so dizzy, he barely made it to the bedroom. His eyes closed in sleep in a matter of seconds. And he was way gone. He fell into a dream about Carol going away on a train. She merely waved good-bye. He saw some people from the Association standing on each side of the train waving good-bye to her.

He slept late on Saturday. Everything was quiet and his head was amazingly clear.Nothing happened around him. His world seemed normal again. The sun was shining. The air was warm. No one came around or made any noise. Once again, his house was his sanctuary. He thought about absolutely nothing at all. He just lay there.

He dragged himself out of bed ad into his study. There he spotted his Bible. It lay there, as usual, on his desk. It was indeed a treasure trove of wisdom. He kept it here and visited it every morning. He sat in front of it and wondered what he would read this morning. He finally chose another passage from the book of Isaiah following the one from last Sunday. He thought highly of the old prophet of Judah. He spoke well to him as a man.

After his reading, he turned on some of his favorite sacred music. When it came to music, he was strictly a connoisseur. He couldn't play to save his life. That had been Carol's job. Now, he had no one to play for him. But he did have his music to be played. It was chants and hymns. It relaxed him like no other music could. It gave him time to meditate on what he had just read. It put him in his zone.

While the music played, he peered out the window and thanked God. He thanked God for all he'd been blessed with, His protection, His will, and His straight gate and narrow way. He thanked Him for Jesus. He thanked Him for the Spirit and the Word. He thanked Him that he had a job in His service. He thanked God for his good health and his friends from the night before. Finally, he thanked God for all of his possessions, music, tv, reading material, etc...

He figured he must be the only person he knew to have in their possession a confessional kneeling altar. He used it for his time for confession of sin. He didn't confess to a priest or pray to Mary or a statue. He confessed his sin directly to God. He also believed he was forgiven., as promised in scripture and he was cleansed from all of his unrighteousness. His confession didn't fall on deaf ears.

But, what would he confess? Was he prepared to confess his bitterness? How about his lack of faith or the laziness he was starting to exhibit? He confessed a few of his latest thoughts? He also confessed some of that stuff he'd seen on tv. He confessed desires in areas he hadn't thought about in a while. But he did feel *kind* of bad about his bitterness and resentment. He confessed confusion, instead, about God's will in this.

He said,

"God, it just doesn't make any sense to me that it would be your will of all things to take her away from Your work here.

"I don't understand it, but I guess I don't have to.But I also know, or am reasonably certain, that the Association doesn't know either.

He found it difficult to pray for them at that point. His anger at them rose again. They were the enemy. He was convinced that God had said for them to continue the work He'd started there. But God said He would continue the work. So, that's what he prayed for, for God to continue the work He'd started there, with or without them.

"God, what am I going to do without her? We had accomplished so much together. Why did you take her away and are you going to bring her back? I feel so alone, and a little afraid."

But, had he prayed that prayer before? He knew it sounded familiar. But, where from?

At what time in his life had he uttered those words?

"Why did you take her away...?"

Who had He taken away? Was someone else taken from him? Yes, someone else had departed at one time in his life. He denied any knowledge of whoso he speaketh. All those old feelings began to resurface.

"I feel so alone."

He went onto finish his intercessory time of prayer. He prayed for his congregation to have listening ears and open hearts and minds. But, was that a prayer for them or for him? He prayed for the volunteers to both lead and follow, to cooperate. He finally prayed for all who would be served that week.

He didn't know what to petition for himself. He wasn't certain he actually wanted what he needed to ask for, peace. Truth was also a scary venture. He feared the repercussions of both. He did, however, ask for help with the music on Sunday. Now, back to the here and now. Back to practical things and not just deep, spiritual requests from an all-knowing God.

He was in the middle of writing his sermon when the phone rang.

"Hello."

"Uh hello. Al Bryant?"

"Yes, can I please ask who's calling?"

"Dennis Klume, I'm the pastor at Eastbrook Baptist Church. How are you today?"

"I'm doing fine, thanks. How are you?"

"I'm well. Thanks for asking. The reason I'm calling is to confirm the date tomorrow for our music minister to assist you at your service."

"I hadn't heard anything about that."

"Oh, well, it was the Association's idea. They mentioned you would be needing someone for a while until they could get someone out there permanently."

'Which will be never' Al thought to himself.

"Uh, thanks. I'm looking forward to it. Just who do I expect to see?"

"Well tomorrow will be our man Tom and another will be there next week."

Why hadn't he been told this before now?

"Thanks. I'll be looking for Tom tomorrow."

"Well, good. It's been a pleasure speaking with you. Have a good day!"

Well, there's an answer to prayer. It was a quick one, too. Now, to finish his sermon. Was it a good idea to continue in Isaiah? Yes, it was, for now. He wrote the sermon and went out to his garden. The weather was cold, so he didn't do much but irrigate in an effort to keep out the water left over from the melted snow in the yard. But that was enough.

He ate lunch, napped, wrote letters, watched tv, ate supper, and called friends, before watching more tv. But, not too late this time.

He got ready for bed at a descent hour, which was a really early for some of his younger compatriots. He was just an old fuddyduddy now. But early to bed would make him healthy (maybe), wealthy (he doubted that), and wise. And wisdom comes about once in a lifetime.

On Sunday, he awoke and got right into the Word. He meditated on some New Testament scripture. Then he threw on a suit and headed off to church. He half-heartedly expected the music man not to show up today. He felt kind of guilty about that. But his expectations of late have not been high enough.

He arrived to see several cars in the parking lot. It was almost as if Carol were still there. It's like nobody knows she's gone. Maybe she's not gone. Has this all been a bad dream? When he woke up this morning, had he been asleep for a week? No, certainly not. But it all looked like last week and the past ten years of Sundays. Wait, is that a cloud he's walking on?

Once inside, reality came on strong in the form of his music man for the day.

"Al, hi, I'm Gary."

"Nice to meet you, Gary. Thanks for coming out."

"No problem. Thanks for having me."

He thought, "I'm not the one having you."

He walked around, greeting parishioners. They all seemed so nice on Sundays. He wondered why some of them had so much trouble on weekdays if they were this nice on Sundays. And did they really mean it when they said it was nice to see him? After all, that wasn't his sentiment upon sight of himself in the mirror that morning.

After all was quiet, he approached his microphone at the pulpit. They all seemed so receiving. Also, he could see every face in the crowd. But, there were one or two he didn't see. It didn't seem to matter anymore. He was all alone now. He had, indeed, become the 'Lone Missionary'. He looked over his notes as he began to speak.

"Good morning, everyone. Although, I really shouldn't say,

'everyone', because I can see some empty seats. I'll try not to take that personally.

A few chuckles.

"We have a special guest today. His name is Gary. He'll be leading the music…

He looked over at the piano to see a stranger there as well. He looked over at Gary. Gary approached the pulpit and whispered that she was his wife.

"Oh, and a guest accompanist as well, Gary's wife. We are indeed blessed to have you both. And, every week, we'll be blessed by a different minister and, probably, accompanist as well."

Boy, were their people unpredictable. He was beginning t feel very much out of control. He didn't know what to expect from week to week. This blindsided him although it really shouldn't matter. This wasn't harming anyone. It just took him by complete surprise. And, what if she wasn't comfortable being here this morning? Was it a 'package deal?' He came out of his thoughts and gave Gary the floor.

He read some scripture and Gary began to sing. He started singing and his wife started playing. He had told Gary that these people preferred the classics for their worship. He took out a hymnal and announced a page number. Everyone turned to it and Al felt like nothing more than a backdrop. Gary proceeded to lead in worship.

Carol had always done a thanksgiving testimonial at this juncture after the worship. But since she always lead the music, it had been a easy transition for her. Also, he wasn't certain that these particular people would even remember what she did. No, it was time for him to institute his own tradition now. But, what would he do? *He* didn't even feel grateful right now.

He went up and started anyway.

He said, "Hello again. I just want today to express my appreciation for all of you and for Gary, and…

He didn't know her name.

"…his wife."

Talk about embarrassing, he would later learn her name was Katy. But, for now, he would remain red-faced. He also did not notice that anyone was offended by the fact that he did not take testimonies like Carol always did. He just did not possess an attitude of gratitude this morning. And he had heard all of their testimonies of gratitude a trillion times. It was always the same things they were thankful for. It never ied from the usual.

Some would be thankful for family, some for jobs, some for church (some of them were just kissing up). A lot of them always just expressed gratitude just for being alive. Others were always thankful for friends and fellowship. But others were honest about their thankfulness for possessions, risking all appearance of greed.

He asked to pray a silent prayer of gratitude followed by confession of sin before the taking of communion. He confessed a lack of gratitude to God, but to no one else. His heart ached. And he began to feel it in his stomach as well. He didn't even feel like being here anymore. He felt unqualified to lead today. He thought maybe he should allow Gary to lead.

After communion, Gary sang a song while his wife played accompaniment. It was a really nice song, maybe an old Southern Gospel something or other, he wasn't certain. But it was about being home with God. Maybe that's exactly what Al wanted.

"Lord, haste the day."

That was his silent prayer.

Then it was time to teach, preach, present. He pulled out the sermon he had written the day before. When he had written it, he had not made the acquaintance of Gary and spouse. He had not been face with the dilemma of testimonies of gratitude. It was a completely different sermon now. It had gone through the possibility of the realization of all this having been nothing more than a dream. Then it went through a fierce bite of reality. He wasn't certain of his readiness to present this.

After it was over, he made his usual announcements:

Recovery meeting that evening Volunteer assignments for Monday Bible study on Wednesday.

He also announced the activities around the Rec Department of another Association. Why couldn't they have their own intermural system? What happened?

Gary introduced his wife, Katy, to a blushing Al. He felt bad because he hadn't known her name. Several people expressed gratitude to the both of them. Being the sweet individual she was, Katy received hugs from many parishioners. Al felt as though he should provide lunch but they had plans. So, he bid them adieu. They said their farewells and proceeded forward. They really were very nice, and gifted as well. He didn't feel as gifted as he thought they were.

At the recovery meeting that evening, a man spoke of resentment. Apparently, it existed as a defect of character for him. Usually, Al didn't feel as though he fit in at these meetings of local drug addicts and alcoholics, among others. He felt like he didn't fit into their circle. But tonight he really could relate to what he heard spoken. He knew resentment only too well.

Resentment and bitterness were eating him up inside. He couldn't get Carol's face out of his head. She seemed like the innocent victim here. She, however, seemed to hold no grudges. How dare she not be angry and hurt by all of this! But, on the other hand, what good would it do for her to feel these things? After all, what's done is done. Or, if she did feel those things, what good would it do to react to it? The responsible parties here were an immovable force. They were like a freight train. They could not be swayed from their evil ways. Now, who's getting carried away?

The next day, he was sitting in office when he got a visitor. The man appeared desperate for help. He was probably about forty but he dressed as though he were an eighteen year old college freshman. He had his hat on sideways and his pants down around his thighs. His watch looked like a cheap knock-off. And he wore a heavy chain around his neck.

He began, "Sir, my name is England, Tony England."

He didn't sound like he had a cockney accent or an urban dialect. So, what, who was he? And, why was he here?

"Can I help you with something?"

"Yes, I mean I hope so," he answered.

"What…"

"Can you help me find a job?"

"What do you need *me* to do?"

"I don't know. I just got to find a job."

"What do you do? And, what have you done so far?"

"Uh, not much, really. Can you help me?"

"I'll certainly try."

The man came in and sat across from Al. It seemed as though every time Al started to do something, this guy just sat back in his chair and seemed to do nothing but watch Al do everything (by himself). Al wasn't like he knew Carol to have been. She had definitely been a soft touch. S, Al emulated him in that every time he quit trying, so did Al. After a while, the guy just seemed to give up altogether. It seemed as though he was just about to get up and walk out when Al addressed him,

"So, why did you come here?"

"I'm trying to find a job."

"Why?"

"What do you mean?"

"Why here?"

"I was told that you could find me one."

"I'll be glad to help you, but what brought you all the way out here?"

"Look, I got to get a job 'cause my family, wife and kids."

The words coming out of his mouth didn't match his clothes or his name.

"Sit down and tell me your problem."

He sat.

"What I really need is money, uh, sir. Me and the Mrs. Got behind on the rent and we're about to get kicked out, and the kids."

"You got a teenager?"

"What? No, they're all under ten, three of 'em."

"Are you in a play, urban theatre maybe?"

"No, what you talkin' 'bout?"

"Your clothes, the way you dress…"

"What, are yahatin'?"

"You listen to rap music?"

"A little bit."

His face was puzzled. Then Al got an idea.

"You a gamer?"

"'Speed Chase', that's my game."

Al had heard of it. It was a violent game played on computer. Lots of people were known to forget everything else for that game.

"Is that why you can't find a job?"

"No."

Al mentioned a place just a few miles away. He said he could either ride with him or follow him out there. Then the guy mentioned he could follow him out but asked if he could get some gas money. Al said that if the guy were sincere, he would front him some gas money. Then he inquired about getting some lunch on the way out. You know, the mission could pay. Al just figured he knew where this was going.

They stopped for gas and the man continued to follow him. He asked if Al would be willing to buy him a pop. Well, he really didn't ask. He just kind of took one up to the counter and expected Al to pay for it. Al ignored him, paid for the gas, and walked out. Frustrated, the guy left the pop on the counter and walked out behind him. When they got back out to the cars, Al told him where they were going.

He got into his car and fell in line behind him. He followed him about a half mile but Al saw in his rear-view mirror the guy had turned left instead of going straight. Al had told him he was taking him out to a production plant that was hiring. He thought he had heard him mumble something about he didn't just give him the money for his rent like they did for others. That's probably why the guy had come in looking like that.

4

Wednesday evening was teaching night. He just got comfortable in the podium and talked about the Bible. He loved teaching from the gospels but tonight he would teach the fruits of the Spirit out of Galatians. He thought they needed to hear that this close to spring when they would begin their service ministry.

He looked out over the crowd and saw everyone he hoped he would see. He did, however, miss that short little time of music Carol always led them in. It didn't seem like it was the same without it, without her. None of this seemed right. Would it ever feel right again? It hadn't felt like he wanted it to in a long time. Someone was missing and it wasn't just Carol.

He was sitting in his office on Thursday when the phone rang.

"Hello, Al Bryant here. How can I be of service?"

"This is Bill Green at the Association. Is your hall available for a Valentine's banquet?"

"Yes, I think it is. I'll check."

He kind of looked at his calendar, not expecting it to have anything in it unless Carol had something and not bothered to tell him about it.

"No, it doesn't seem as though we are busy that evening."

"Great, thanks. We'll have a meeting about it. What's a good day for you?"

Oh, great, a meeting.

"Let's do Monday."

"We'll be there. Oh, and, by the way, How many you got signed up for basketball there?"

He had to check.

"Uh, actually, two."

"Did you play it up at all?"

"Well, I announced it but I was looking at several people that I just didn't see as having any interest."

"What about the kids? They like to play."

"Don't you have enough athletes already?"

He meant 'wanna be' athletes.

"I just don't think you gave it a fair chance."

He was right. Al didn't feel like taking that on. If he had found a lot of people to be interested, he'd have to get them all signed up. And then he'd probably have to provide transportation and it would just become its own thing. He just didn't have time.

He did announce it again on Sunday but with no real vigor as before as well. He only wanted to see the really dedicated go out for it. Yeah, right, like anybody would be motivated by his bleak announcement. But he did manage to give everyone the heads up that the Valentine's banquet would be held there this year. Did 60-year old widow Mabel Harrington just smile at him? He hoped not. Well, anyway, on with it all.

Come Monday, Bill Green showed up with a few others. They were all back-stabbing greed mongers. That's all he could think about. These were the people who had downsized Carol right in the back. Ouch! That hurt just thinking about it. Look at them, four of them with pen in hand. What on earth would they talk about?

They could talk about bringing Carol back to work there. He thought about bringing it up. What could they say, no? What's the worst could happen? But, that's not what they were coming for. They were coming to plan a Valentine's Day banquet. It would be free for the parishioners of the area. Big deal! A big, romantic evening with dinner and probably someone to sing and play.

He checked the coffee machine and found some pastry someone provided. The table was clean and he hoped, or he didn't really care, if there were enough chairs. There were ten. If more than that showed up, he didn't want to have the meeting anyway, so what to do if...? There was no way he was retrieving more chairs. They were adults. They could get their own.

He heard people at the door. He looked and noticed them arriving one at a time. He counted probably six. Wouldn't you know there was plenty of room. No more excuses. Meeting is on. They slowly walked around the room as though searching, for something. Really? Could they not find the table? This was the conference room, not the cafeteria. But they found it and they sat. Wait, what about the coffee? Were they expecting him to serve them?

No, he wasn't going to do that. He sat down and everyone talked among themselves for a few minutes. Did they not all ride together? How much more could they possibly have to talk about? Oh, wait, that's right, they're church people. All these people ever do is talk. When all is said and done, more is said than done. Now, who's gonna start this meeting so they can get it over with? Oh, well, I guess it's up to yours truly.

"Ladies and Gentlemen, welcome and thank you all for coming today.

He pointed toward the table by the wall.

"There's coffee and donuts.

One woman stood up but looked at him unbelievably.

"I trust you all had a...

He thought 'Good? Safe?Fun?Interesting?

"a half-way decent drive.

Hey all appeared judgmental and condemning. Then one spoke.

"Al, we're here to plan an Association-wide Valentine's party. So, let's get started."

Bill Green interjected, "How about a tour of the cafeteria so we can begin planning?"

They all agreed and stood to walk out. Some poured coffee and snagged Danish on the way out.

Al led the way as he began to talk about it.

"We have plenty of room in there for about 300-500 people. That's generally the number we serve daily."

There were looks.

The perpetrator of one such look spoke:

"How are we supposed to enjoy a romantic evening in a place where is fed such people?"

Al replied to…that remark, "Just like they did in the Bible in the story Jesus told of the guy who sent his servant out to the streets to find guests for his party."

Bill then said, "It's fine, just fine. Just clean it up and all is well."

Al was almost offended. But it occurred to him they cleaned it up every day anyway. So, what difference would one more time make? Probably none.

"Now", Bill continued, "let's talk decorations."

They all surveyed the room, some with looks of derision, some with disgust, others with that 'no way' look.

"Balloons, I say Valentine balloons", Al remarked.

"Great, the usual then, but when?" Bill asked.

Al was surprised that everybody didn't already know.

"The volunteers will take care of it", Al offered.

"Now", Bill said, "let us plan a date."

"How about February 14th?" Al asked as his question for the day.

"Yes", Fred answered, "I think that's good."

All seemed satisfied.

Then someone asked, "What about tickets?"

It was DelorasFinkam. She was the secretary at First Church.

"Shall I take care of it again?" she asked.

Al didn't want her to because she had a tendency to sell tickets at her church first. That's the way she'd done it the last two years.

"Deloras," Al began, "why don't you allow someone else to take that burden this year?"

With a straight face she answered, "No burden at all."

The last couple of years have seen the people at her church get first dibs at seats long before anyone else had a chance.

He decided not to press the issue. Who knows, maybe the third time is the charm. Besides, if she pulled those old tricks again, it would be enough to use against her ever doing tickets again. Will she be up to her old tricks? Probably! She would take the tickets to her church and offer them there first. And the other churches wouldn't see any until she was ready to share.

"How many?" she asked.

"350", he answered.

Six churches and the mission church, 50 a piece.

Fred offered, "Everyone, go ahead and make the announcement, but allow over 50."

Everyone agreed.

Okay, meeting adjourned.

He went out Tuesday to announce the banquet and the softball league. He went around spreading the word. Some showed interest in one or the other. He announced to all that they were waiting on tickets to be printed. Some showed interest in playing softball. He said they could sign up at the mission and the season would start in March. Most of all, he enjoyed the visiting.

Then he went out to see Bob and Alice, the family he had visited with Carol. They were the first couple that had come to mind. He went out to their home and he realized that they may be expecting Carol. They probably had not forgotten she was gone, but what if they had? He found himself in the midst of that fear quite often recently. He was just so tired of having to deal with that on a daily basis.

He just kept having to reannounce her departure over and over again, almost on her own volition. It was like it was her idea and not theirs. If only she had protested, just a little. But she didn't. He did, though. It was enough for both of them except that he felt all alone in his protest. They got rid of her. She left willingly. And he was left with his feelings.

Two of the kids, a boy and a girl, ran out to meet him at the car. They didn't even seem to look for Carol. But they knew him. They called him by name. When he got out, they hugged him and announced mom was in the house. Dad was working on a job that day. That was certainly good news for them. Alice looked out the door with her youngest hanging on her leg. He saw the oldest boy, Bobby, playing on a swing in the yard. Alice took her ankle biter in her arms and went out to greet him.

"Al", she began, "what brings you all the way out here?"

"I just came out to see how you'll are doing. I understand Bob's working?"

"Yeah, he got a job going to go on for a few days, pays good and we need the money."

It just about seemed like she was apologizing that he wasn't at home just then.

"That's good, Alice. You doing okay, and the kids?"

"You still home schooling the kids?"

Yes, I'm still doing my best but it ain't as easy as I thought."

"Well, if there's anything…"

This really was Carol's specialty.

"I came out to let you and Bob know about a Valentine's banquet we're having on Valentine's Day at the Mission."

"That sounds lovely, Al, but I don't think we could get a sitter. Thank you, though."

"Well, if you should change your mind…"

Should he tell her about the softball league? Would Bob even be interested? He played once when their Association had a league. But he figured he'd rather see Bob working if it came down to a choice between the two. Alice was right about them needing the money. He thought about the oldest boy, Bobby, playing in the youth soccer league. There was just so much he wanted forthis family. They were always so nice. And, they were faithful in attendance at church. If only there existed more like them.

On Wednesday, he announced the plans for the banquet and that they would have fifty tickets for twenty-five couples. He didn't know for certain when the tickets would be printed. He didn't know when they'd tell him they were ready. He also wondered if he should trust Deloras. She had been upset as it is that the banquet wouldn't be at her church again this year.

He taught them that night on faith:

"Folks, we're coming out of Genesis tonight. We're studying the faith of Father Abraham. Abraham is just one of several mentioned in Hebrews eleven, what is known as the 'Hall of Faith'. It says, 'it was accounted righteousness to him.' He had several opportunities in his life to learn to trust in God. Tonight, I'm going to talk about three of them.

"First of all is the incident when God broke the news to the ninety year old that he would soon be a father. Abram, as he was known at the time, found himself in disbelief due to his age, as anybody would. Abram had difficulty trusting God on this one because he had no reference point to draw upon. We, however possess the benefit of 20/20 hindsight. We have read of all that God has done, so we believe.

"Yet Abram had what Jesus would later refer to as a mustard seed of faith. That's all that was required. That's all he needed. He just needed to know that God was, although Moses hadn't even been born yet, let alone had God said that He was 'I Am'. But all that Abram need to know was that He Was. A mustard seed of faith was all that was required for him to believe God's promise, no matter how crazy it seemed.

"So, the first of the types of faith Abram was challenged with was simply to have a mustard seed of faith. The Lord spoke of this in the gospels. He spoke it both to His disciples and to us at the same time. He said that all we needed was that little bit of faith.

Any more than that was unnecessary and would probably just get in the way anyway.

"But the second type of faith a trust in God that He's on the throne no matter what. Abraham's brother had passed and he took in his nephew Lot. Lot inherited, a lot, of value from his father.

Chuckles…

"Pardon the play on words there. But both had great possessions and about a hundred servants apiece. It got so bad the servants were fighting among themselves about whose sheep were whose.

"It got so bad they had to split up. Sound familiar? Ever know anyone like that? Things get so bad, a split is the only way? Anyway, they decided together no longer to be together. Abraham, though, allowed Lot to choose which he wanted. One was better and, of course, Lot chose the better of two. But, Abraham probably knew that he would.

"Abraham didn't trust Lot to do it any other way. It didn't matter, though, what Lot chose. We are not expected to trust others. We are, instead, expected to trust God no matter what others do. Jesus didn't trust anyone but His Father. He even had foreknowledge of what others would do to Him. He knew, for instance, of the betrayal at the kiss of Judas.

"First of all, all that's required of us is something as small as a mustard seed of faith. But, when was the last time you heard of a tree being uprooted or a mountain being moved? I don't think it's ever happened. But that little mustard seed of faith is all we need. And then to trust God no matter what others do rids us of the need to rely on the trustworthiness of others.

"Do you know what I consider the ultimate trust in another person? I think that's to trust them with your child. There are probably a select few people we trust for the care of our child. We put that person through a lot of scrutiny before handing over our precious…one. If it were your car, it would (should) be easier just to accept that it didn't matter what someone else did because we trust God.

"But with our children that's very different, because it does matter what they do. However, that's one of those times we trust God to protect our child. Trust Him overall to just be God no matter what others may do to us. I'm certainall of you fathers of teen girls know of that if your daughters are dating. Trust God and hope for the rest.

"Finally, there's a sacrificial faith where we are expected to believe until it hurts.One day, God called on Abraham to sacrifice his son (sound familiar?) that he had been promised. It didn't make any earthly sense, this request. God had promised Abraham as many descendents as the sands of the sea shore and the stars in the sky. But, now God was calling on him to lay this promise on the altar? Does this remind you of anything?

"Of course it does. God would do this very thing with His own Son. And the fact that Isaac was but twelve years of age is significant in that it is the age that many cultures consider the last age of innocence. It's the year before the onset of adulthood. The Native Americans refer to it as the rite of passage in which a young man must prove himself a man.

"I think the funniest line in the Bible is in this passage. Father and son are walking up the hill. Isaac can see the wood for the altar and the knife as well. But, what of the sacrificial lamb? Father pats son on the shoulder and reassures him that God will provide the sacrifice. But poor, trusting Isaac, he doesn't have a clue. It's like an inside joke between God and Abraham.

"But then, Abraham did as directed and put his son on the altar. It was the vary place a sacrificial animal should be as opposed to a twelve year old. He was still at the age of innocence. The joke about it not being a sacrifice at thirteen may have more truth in it than we know. It wouldn't have been a sacrifice at all at thirteen. It would have been retribution. Parents of teens will understand that one. But, anyway, the sacrifice of Christ was dependent upon His innocence.

"Yet, Isaac just lay there and trusted his father. Why? Because he witnessed his father trusting his Father. Abraham set the example. If your children see your belief, they will believe. You know how good faith is, the peace of knowing God is on His throne no matter what and even that mustard seed of faith. But, especially the sacrificial faith. You know the blessing and you can share it."

He finished up and the service ended. Some guys approached him for information regarding the basketball league. Five couples expressed interest in the banquet. And he even received kudos on his lesson. He watched them all leave slowly and he regarded his night as an accomplishment. So, he stopped and got a burger on the way home.

A week and a day later, he got a phone call from the printer. They wanted him to know that the banquet tickets were ready. He inquired as to whether he needed to pick them up. They said no, that the person who picked them up just thought you should get a call to inform you that the tickets were ready. He wondered if that meant she was ready to bring his tickets over. So, he called her to see if she was ready for him to pick up his tickets. She said she would tell him when it was time.

As a matter of fact, she informed him that as soon as she managed to commit all the tickets for her church, she would let him know. It was the same as the last two years. She would wait until the members of her church had the time they needed to decide if they wanted the tickets. He tried to make the point that he had several people interested at the mission. But she wouldn't budge on it.

In the next week, several people called to ask about tickets. One said he had been told the tickets would be at the mission. The fact that the printer had called him was getting out around the Association. Everyone seemed under the impression that because the printer called him that he had the tickets. He tried to figure out a way to inform them that Deloras had the tickets. That would sove a lot of problems but it would probably cause even more.

It got down to four days before the banquet. Still, only one church had tickets that were not committed. But she still held out for more confirmations. Something had to give. But, what could he do?

He was in no position to put his foot down. They had done nothing in the last two years. It just turned into a bad experience both times.

However, someone did put their foot down, her pastor. He tired of hearing her whining efforts. But all the while she feigned effort, her attempt was at the purpose of hoarding the banquet. So, at his insistence, she handed over the tickets and he took them around to the other churches, including the mission. All the churches, including the mission, began distributing tickets. But they just couldn't get them around fast enough.

In the end, 180 out of 350 were distributed around the Association. But, 180 would make for a nice time if all confirmations showed up. It got to just one day before the banquet when they stopped giving them out. That was to give the volunteers in the kitchen time to prepare the meals as well as fix up the dining room. All seemed at ease now.

Then a familiar face came back around. It was the young friend of Carol, the musician, seeking work doing musical entertainment. Al saw him this time, though, as a possible source of entertainment for the banquet. The young fellow hemmed and hawed but Al did not bow to his whims so he accepted the offer of $100.00 and ran with it. He did, however, mention that he couldn't promise to play all of his greatest hits for that price. Whatever!

On the night of…, the number of tables had been decreased from 175 to ninety. The floor looked nice with all the newly available space. There would certainly be less bumping of chairs together during the evening. And with the lights turned low for ambiance… The volunteers did a good job of setting up for the banquet. He just hoped the participants make it worth their efforts.

The dinner was scheduled for seven o'clock. But at 6:45, there was only one couple, the pastor of First church and his beloved. They would be the only couple for fifteen minutes before a couple from the mission showed up. In the following fifteen minutes, only four other couples made their confirmations shown. Then, Delorasand her husband arrived close to 7:30.

Al directed his volunteers to proceed with the service of food. The young musician complained that his audience wasn't big enough to warrant any serious effort into his performance. He was insulted they would arrive in such small numbers, like they were here to see him in the first place. He just didn't think he could play under such conditions.

Al said, "Fine, no play, no pay."

He proceeded with some borrowed tunes from days of old. The table servers served as three other couples arrived. One participant said that someone he talked to in the parking lot changed their minds when they noticed the low turn-out. And they mentioned something else about telling others before they wasted their evening driving out here. It was Fred who told him of this. One of the other couples who just arrived included the guy in charge of the softball team.

Al looked out over the sadly low turn-out and considered scripture. Jesus told a story about a man who invited several people to a feast and they bugged out with all kinds of excuses. So, he sent out his servants to the streets to invite all types of what would today be considered "undesirables". That gave Al an idea.

He excused himself from the guests. After all, he was alone anyway. He proceeded to his office, sat down, and dialed the phone.

"Hello", Alice answered.

"Alice, this is Al at the mission. How are things tonight?"

"Oh, just fine I guess, just sitting down to dinner."

He thought for a second he was too late, but he said it anyway,

"Would you and Bob like to attend the Valentine's Banquet this evening?"

"Thank you, Al, but there'd be no way we could get someone to watch the kids…"

"No need. There's plenty of room for all of you."

"Why, what would I do with this dinner I cooked?"

"You all have leftovers for dinner on Saturdays anyway, don't you?"

"Well, yes, but, well, I don't know."

"Talk it over with Bob and if you all decide to grace us with your presence tonight, just come on over."

He hung up feeling good about it.

He called a few others and promptly returned to the banquet room. He noticed Deloras speaking with her pastor. Al approached their table as the Master of Ceremonies.

"Deloras, I don't think you need to serve on this committee anymore."

"Pastor, I really don't mind…"

"Well, Deloras, I do mind. You've done nothing but impede progress on this event since you first began serving on this committee. Look for yourself at the low turnout. There could've (should've) been a lot more if you had just distributed the tickets as soon as you picked them up."

"Pastor, our church has served as the social center of this association for years. We can't just…"

"We"re called to reach out to those Jesus called us to minister to in Acts 1:8. Besides, our church is not the social center of the Association. This mission is. The matter is of no consequence. Good evening!"

He thanked Al as he passed by him in retreat to his own table. Al returned the expression of gratitude. That would certainly change things for the better.

Well they showed up. Bob, Alice, the kids and all the others he had called. And some of them invited others as well. The volunteers began setting up more tables and chairs. But there had been plenty of food to go around. His primadonna musician complained again that this was not what he signed up for. But Al reminded that nothing had indeed been signed, not even the agreement for 100 dollars. He thought it best to start out with some songs the kids might like.

The fellow who had been so concerned with the softball sign-ups did, of course, manage to corner Al. When Al told him of the fifteen who had signed up, he looked as though he couldn't understand why

Al hadn't just signed them up in the first place. He went on to say he thought he could form a team in the league with that many. Had he done it right at all?

AL said he would get the forms for him later but for now he had a banquet to host. It was just that simple to walk away from this young fellow. He walked around and greeted everyone, thanking them all for coming out on such short notice. Deloras and a couple of others complained of the originally uninvited guests. But it didn't matter. Her pastor seemed very pleased with the turn-out as he mingled among the people, one and all. What an incredible evening this had turned out to be.

For the remainder of the year, he performed his duties the best he knew how. In the spring, he led his volunteers in service projects around the Association. They gave out food, served meals, gave out clothes, even participated in the softball league in another association. In the summer, they held a series of church day camps and Backyard Bible clubs where they shared the gospel.

In the fall, the mission hosted a revival and then they held a fall festival to offset Halloween. That's when they kicked off the holiday celebrations that would go through to January 1st. That would include a bug Thanksgiving dinner for the community, his playing Santa, giving out gifts to kids, and not to mention Caroling. He worked around all the politics and back-biting, not to mention the nagging he received from people at the Association regarding the reports.

5

The politics would continue unhindered. The reports would be requested and required periodically. There were the monthly safety and health reports. Then there were the quarterly budget reports. And next were the semi-annual ministry preliminary reports. And, last but certainly not least, the annual ministry reports. And there was the guy who oversaw the church sports. He called him about golf, volleyball, basketball, and all other recreational leagues around the surrounding associations. Holidays also received special attention. There were always plenty of people available to tell him how to do his job.

And it would, of course, keep happening that every time he sat down to fill out a report, someone would call. And not just any type of someone but always someone from the Association. If they wanted these reports, you'd think they would stop calling just at the time he sat down to fill them out. But, what got done would get done and he dared them to call and ask. And they did call and ask, threatening to close down the mission if he didn't get them done. They weren't actual threats, though, just innuendos.

The health and safety reports were done monthly but they were just one sided forms. It was just a matter of checking off yes and no boxes. He had learned about those little check-off boxes in school when girls would write notes to him asking if he liked them and to check the yes box or the no box. But there were probably about twenty to thirty boxes on *this*checklist. He put it on a clip board and went pencil in hand to the kitchen and other areas as well. He found questions about the temperature of the freezer, the rat traps in the food pantry, the moth balls in the clothes closet, and several others.

He would prefer to pass this one off to a volunteer. Once again, he was realizing just how bad Carol was at delegating. If she had only delegated this responsibility to one of them, they would probably still be expected to complete it even today. But, instead, he would have to choose a responsible party to follow him around while he performed the actual inspection and also taught someone how to fill out the tiny, one-sided paper that the Association seemed to find so incredibly important.

Why did she insist on doing everything herself? She always disagreed with him regarding the expectations put upon the volunteers. She always said she didn't feel like they felt appreciated when given orders. But he felt like they (he and her) were responsible for the day-day activities of the mission and that the volunteers were to work under their direction. Whenever he expressed that opinion, she expressed the fear of losing volunteers. That was never something he concerned himself with.

He took his clipboard to the kitchen and chose a woman named Gertrude to assist him. She'd been there a few years and seemed to always be in charge of the kitchen.

"Gertrude, can you assist me?"

He thought that her name would go just right at the top of that schedule.

"Sure, Al, just let me finish up over here."

She was preparing lunch.

"As soon as you're ready."

She finished up and stood before him. The others seemed puzzled at his intentions.

They proceeded to the freezer.

"Gertrude, "he said as he pointed at the thermostat," see that temperature?"

She seemed nervous as she looked at it.

"What's it say?" he continued.

"27 degrees, Fahrenheit."

"Good, he said as he showed her the check-off list.

"See right there where it asks if the temperature is 32 degrees or below?"

"Yes,…sir."

He checked the yes box. And then he thought 'But, no, Gertrude, I don't like you in that way.'

"Good, now, what's next?"

She walked all over the building with him, watching, listening, and eventually checking boxes. Before it was over, h had successfully taught her how to complete this task by herself. And he thought,

'Maybe if he left the forms in the kitchen, that she would pick up the task.'

But, what if she didn't take the hint? So, he shared with her his intentions. She seemed completely beside herself. It would seem as though he were asking too much. All he really needed was for her to be his eyes and hands for this monthly task, nothing else. He wasn't asking her to preach or anything. But, what if she made a mistake? That could come back and bite him… But, wouldn't it be funny? Yeah, this was a good idea.

Now, as for the other reports, well, he would have to do them himself. They involved things he was specifically responsible for. He hated dealing with the money. He knew that if he didn't spend all the money they gave him in the budget, they wouldn't give him that much money again and he might actually need it next quarter. It was better to have too much than not enough. But he can't be careless in regard to reporting either. Frivolous expenditures had a tendency to raise eyebrows.

The quarterly budget report had to be out n time for churches utilize in their quarterly business meetings. Each congregation needed to know how much money they were going to give to the mission. Oh, there was always complaining and plenty of it. There was always at least one of the churches that wanted a detailed view of the expenditures of the mission. But only the Association office held the need to know on that one. They could, however, request such information from said office. But, for some unknown reason, they always made a direct request for I from Al. Imagine that and why.

But he never gave them those details because he knew it was only a matter of time for them. They could talk all they wanted to about how their refusal to donate would certainly be the end of things for the mission. Yet, if that happened, all the people who depended on the mission would have to begin attending the churches in the Association for help and they certainly wouldn't want that. So, this vicious cycle of back biting and accusations would continue on for the unforeseeable future.

So, he sits down with his morning coffee. He turns on his computer and activates the budget software. He then proceeded, after taking a sip of coffee, to fill I the blanks on the form in front of him on the screen. All the numbers have been recorded on the digital worksheets, also on the software. He takes another sip and considers a pastry he once knew, oh so short a time ago, in the very same kitchen where he had attained a hot (now getting cold) cup of coffee. Should he seek a reunion with the cheese Danish?

Upon completion of the budget report, and the Danish, he breathed a sigh of relief as he emailed the dastardly thing to the Association office. And, of course, he promptly attached the 'Read Only' rider to it. Not really, he just didn't look forward to hearing about how he had spent so much money on this and not enough on that. If he went so far as to email a copy to the IRS, they might have some interesting thoughts about his allowable expenditures.

But their response wouldn't be immediate. And it's lunch time, well, not quite, but close. Wander around the mission and delegate. It was his sweet revenge on her for not fighting harder for her job. He smiled as he thought about how easily she just stepped out of her place and left him all alone. But, was it her he was thinking about or someone else? Anyway, he delegated like she never could. He had volunteers actually working. But, would they return tomorrow? He hoped not. But, wait! What was he thinking, no volunteers? Oh, they'll be back, maybe.

The semi-annual preliminary was just that, *preliminary*. It preceeded the annual report by six months. And it brought with it the idea that we do not wait a whole year before reporting progress or lack of…progress. It wasn't like anybody looked at it anyway. It went to someone's desk and not being the big one, which they only looked upon if they had to see something on it anyway. So, if he failed completion of such report, or if he did not, who would even notice?

This report told of numbers served, numbers saved, how many joined their happy congregation, just a bunch of head counting. It reminded Al of King David's census. Besides, he knew that heaven rejoiced over the salvation of one single soul. But, they seemed to need to justify all the money given to the mission What if a thousand made decisions but only a hundred of those were authentic? They didn't inquire of those numbers. But, isn't that what Jesus told of it the parable of the sower? A LOT OF people who came through here heard the gospel. A lot of them received it. But troubles in life choked it out.

But God was always there, just like He said He would be. And He was always kicking Al in the behind about his resentments, not to mention his attitude. But, how did God feel about what those people did to Carol? And, speaking of Carol, how did He feel about her lack of desire to delegate tasks to volunteers? Did God enjoy Himself at the banquet last year? He's certainly welcome this year. Easter was a hoot. It's the only holiday where we actually celebrate Him. That even includes Christmas.

He began to put a system together. It was one that only he could understand. It involved his schedule on a day-day platform. Mondays would consist of work and monitoring the center. Tuesdays would be visitation days. Wednesdays would be spent in preparation for all of his ministries. Thursdays would be paperwork days. On Fridays, you may not see him at all, kind of a play day, of sorts. Saturdays would be spent at home gardening and writing his sermon. Sunday would be morning worship and the usual recovery ministry at night. True, following this schedule might make him a bit predictable, but only if one took the time to watch and learn.

Then something disrupted his system and his thinking. It proved to be both unexpected and terribly tragic. As he pondered on his schedule and his duties as wl as his anger and resentment, a call came into the mission. This type of thing hadn't happened in a long while. The State Police were on the other end.

"I see", Al replied as he hung up the phone.

It seems two local boys had been swinging on a rope at the lake. They had been dropping from the rope into the cold water below. One of the boys, however, hit his head on a rock. They had been on spring break from school. None of their prents were aware they'd gone there today. But the other young man lacked the strength to pul him up from the water. A dark spot of blood filled the water hole. They had not done anything wrong, except for not informing any of their parents where they were going. None the less, neither deserved to die. Al felt a deep sense of loss, as he had once before. The boy was 13 years old.

He made an unexpected visit to Bob and Alice. But he just sat in his car as he stared at an empty tire swing hanging from a tree in the yard. He pictured a little boy who at one time played in that very swing. All he knew at that moment was that these fine people had lost a beloved son. He was their oldest. He h been a beautiful, blue-eyed boy. He was here yesterday. He was gone just a day later and forever after. Al slowly got out of his car. The place felt different already. Why had this happened? Why does it ever happen? Someone is here one day and gone the next.

Alice looked out the screen door as she always does. Her youngest was at her heel, as usual. Where was everyone else? They were probably gathered inside. The other young boy involved had told the police where Bobby lived (had lived). He would later become just like a son to Bob and Alice. But for right at this moment, it was up to Al to find words of comfort and consolation for a grieving family. It had just been four years ago that two other families had lost children in an auto accident, sixteen and seventeen. They had been driving late at night, too fast on a wet, windy road. The car rolled several times.

"Bob, Alice", he began sadly.

The kids all appeared very sad. The oldest girl was crying. Bob consoled her just like a good daddy would.

"Thanks for coming out, Al", Bob managed through his little girl's sobbing.

"Is there anything you'll need I can do for you?"

Al meant that with all possible sincerity.

"Can you do the eulogy?" Alice asked through her own tears.

Al agreed and two days later, they were burying this young lad. They had told him what they wanted him to say. It seems he had a favorite story in the Bible that his grandpa, who had passed a few years back, used to tell him. It was the story of Shadrach, Meshak, and Abedniggo. He had enjoyed the part where they were sent into the furnace and the soldiers got burned up instead. And then, once inside, everybody witnessed a fourth person in there with them. He liked to think that was Jesus. Grandpa said Jesus was always with us no matter what. So, they buried Robert Henry Clark, Jr. next to his grandpa.

"I honestly thought I would go first," Bob sad to Al afterward.

He continued, "Now, I just don't know."

"Bob, somehow I know what you mean."

"You do? How?"

"I've been there."

He received hugs from all the family members, including the little one. Although, this one wasn't sure about all of this.

Folks came from miles around to offer their condolences. And they brought food, as folks always do in these circumstances. Other churches contributed as well. Youth groups showed up to offer support. Alice couldn't stop crying as she was comforted by guests. Then everyone heard a tiny voice.

"Where's Bobby?"

It was their youngest. He seemed to be searching the house for his big brother. Al picked him up and told him Bobby was in heaven.

"Oh," was his reply.

Al called Carol to tell her. She met him when he was just a year old. He let her hold him. She later taught him how to sing. Al never could figure out why the child had liked her so much, as boyish as he was. When he came into her Sunday School class at five, he spoke of her all the time. Otherwise, he was always so energetic and hyper. Girls seemed to like him and he might have been popular in middle school, but now they'll never know. All he ever wanted to do was play and have a good time. But, that's what got him.

"Carol, are you okay?"

There had been a second or two of silence at the other end.

"Yes, I guess so. That's just so sad."

"I know. I just can't believe it."

"What happened?"

"He and another young man went out to the lake without permission. They were swinging on the tire swing and jumping in the water. Bobby hit his head on a rock."

"Who was the other boy?"

"Erin Wilson. He's kind new around here."

"What did he do?"

"He ran up and told some guys who worked out there. They got there and saw him in the water face down."

"Oh, my. How's the family?"

He told her about the little one. She giggled and it sounded like she was crying a little too. He said that little one would probably be Alice's saving grace. Bob didn't seem to be believing it yet. The brother and sister were both very sad. He expressed that he feared depression would set in for one and resentment for the other. They discussed with how one could possibly cope with having to bury their offspring. One's children are supposed to bury their parents. Bob and Alice may blame one another. Bob would accuse her of not watching the kids. Alice would say Bob should have spent more time with him. But they both knew what the real problem was. Bobby was always what is so often referred to as 'the milkman's kid".

Alice remembered giving birth to him. And she knew for certain that Bob was the only man she had ever been with. It's just that Bobby neither looked or acted like either of them. But he did resemble one of her cousins. It was one of those familial phenoms that make you go "hmm". She couldn't remember what the doctor called it but it had something to do with the genetic pool. And out of that pool swam a cancerous cell. Bobby had been diagnosed three years ago with Arterial Sclerosis, a disease of the arteries.

They never agreed as to how to properly care for their son, although their doctor gave them specific instructions. He took medication that Bob did not enforce the use of. Yet, Alice insisted he take it. However, she did try to give him his space. She didn't hound him in other areas of care like Bob did. Sometimes, it seemed to her that Bob had been conducting some kind of science experiment with their son. It was like he wanted to test whether the boy actually needed it or not. It costs a lot of money. Alice didn't care about that. If Bobby had died of the disease, as he had been expected to do before his fifteenth birthday, Bob might have been guilty of medical neglect. But, as it was, he blamed Alice.

6

His second summer without Carol began with lots to do. Churches from around the Association began their "Lake Park" ministry, where they alternated weeks doing backyard Bible clubs and held big cook-outs for the families on Saturday. The pastors delegated men from their respective churches to lead chapel services on Sundays. They ministered to both area families and vacationers alike. That lake was a very popular place in the summer. People showed up there from miles around for a week or two at a time.

Most of the supplies came out of the mission warehouse. Some of the volunteers came out of there as well. When it was his congregation's turn, which it was twice a summer, Al went out there every day with the exception of Monday, Thursday, and Sunday. He wanted very badly to preach out there one Sunday but it was difficult since he never who would be leading the music at the mission church from Sunday to Sunday. He also had to stay in on Mondays and Thursdays in an effort to get work done, like reports. And even on those days he was fielding calls from the very same Association members who wanted them so badly. From now on, however, he would do this job his way.

First Baptist Church got weeks one and eight. A few years prior, our Miss Deloras had been in charge of that team from there. But her focus was on the locals she knew personally. They had been required to arrive an hour early for recruiting but she would try to find houses she recognized or ones that appeared to house *important* people. Needless to say, they never had a big turnout. And she really did not motivate her people joyfully.

But, this year would be different. The pastor and his wife would be leaders of this year's team. He got a little over-excited and recruited from outside the boundary markings set by the Association. His wife utilized her amazing Sunday School skills to tell the Bible stories. He enjoyed leading the games. He was a really big kid. He also ran the grill on Saturday. He just had a really great time. He even found himself preaching in shorts at church. He found himself very fond of this para-church ministry stuff. And evangelism was right up his alley. He even talked about buying real estate out there. But his wife reminded him that they still had to finish paying off the one they currently occupied.

Lonesome River church had week two but they delegated week nine to the Mission because that would be their camp week. That was the church that Carol had attended before she began employment at the mission twelve years ago. It hadn't changed in twelve years, maybe a little. The pastor had been there only about three years but the deacons remained the same. They didn't even seem to age much. They always had the same number of teens and children at any given time. But, of course, they changed. They went to school, graduated, worked, and became parents themselves.

So the mission got two weeks, although it was the last one in line. Al relished the idea of having so much to do to keep him out of the office during the day. He went out to the park and enjoyed telling the stories to the kids and running the grill on Saturday. But he called the college for his Sunday speaker. He also counted on them for a song leader. Those college kids loved this kind of stuff. And they were good at it. He thought he'd even enjoy hosting a mission team from there to come out for one of these weeks, at least to help out one of the churches. The gospel excited him. Then he started about participating on other weeks.

At one point he stopped and looked out across the lake at the very spot where Bobby had lost his young life. His blood had washed out. It was like Bobby himself went that way. He had gone on down the river. Al began thinking about the cycle of life. Bobby's had been but a young life, snuffed out earlier than expected. But, he was headed that direction anyway. Yet, Bob thought differently of it and Alice prepared for it. But, who could have prepared for this? This was a warning for him not only to pray for this family, but to give them eternal hope.

He had to get them out here, to this place. But, how ever could he get Alice here with the kids? And would Bob come out on Saturday? Alice would come if she brought the kids, even the little one who would turn 2 years old soon. Bob would certainly come out for free eats on Saturday. Al had two weeks to convince them. Deloras would hate it but Carol would be all about it. He knew that Jesus would love this family and they fell in line with Acts 1:8. Okay, next Tuesday they would get a visit.

To Alice he would say, "Bring the kids."

To Bob he would offer, "Free eats."

But to pray first. He knew what he had to do.

But for now he told Bible stories to kids three days a week. He came out on Tuesday and told of Noah. He gave the story of David and Goliath on Wednesday. And, he told of Zachaeus on Friday. These kids were the best, most attentive audience he'd had in a while. But he wouldn't dare forget the gestures. He made the motion of waves for Noah as the kids (and adults) joined in. He swung his sling around for David and he led everyone to look up in a tree for Zachaeus He had so much fun, he forgot about other things.

But those other things were waiting for him at the office. While he helped people gather supplies for the ministry, the Association office called to check up on stuff for camp, summer retreats, golf, and of course the preliminary report. He didn't think it was time for that yet. Yes, June had come and gone but they were still in the midst of ministry. Well, he sat down to it once his team was loaded and ready to go, but guess who called? The Ministry Lend Out Committee called to inquire as to who was leading music there on Sunday. He said he wouldn't know until Sunday. They indicated it was his responsibility to choose his own interim every week.

'Don't you want your report?'

He proceeded out to Bob and Alice's to invite the kids to Bible Clubs and Bob and Alice to the cook-out. But, only Alice was home along with the kids. The first thing he noticed when he pulled into the drive was the empty swing out front. It was once very frequently occupied by their oldest, Bobby.

"Hey, Reverand," Jimmy, the second oldest (now oldest) son said as he ran by him.

"Hey, Jimmy," was his response.

He approached the front door.

He knocked and was invited inside.

"Alice," he started as he slowly made his way into their home.

He continued, "I've come to invite your two children to Bible clubs down by the lake.

Then it occurred to him they would be in eyeshot of where Bobby had died.

"But, if you would rather…not, I understand. It may be kind of…"

"What kind of stuff are they going to be doing out there, sir," Jenny asked.

"Fun stuff," was his immediate reply.

Alice agreed to take the kids. Al informed that he probably would not go out on Monday. And he also warned her that the location of their Bible club had a view of the place where her son had died. She said it would be alright, that he was no longer there. He was in heaven. And, what happened there was an accident. It would not bring about bad memories. She said it might even inspire her to share the gospel with the kids out there and maybe hers would find Christ.

"It could only be good," she concluded.

On Monday, the team from the mission arrived, on time, to get their supplies for the ministry on the lake. He wished he could go with, but he had to work around the mission on that day. He had to check on the volunteers and their schedules to make sure the schedules matched those of the volunteers. He had also been relegated to security monitor. He had to perform monitoring tasks to be sure there were no stragglers loitering about. Also, he felt like he needed to be sure that everyone was getting along okay.

They left out and he went…to…his…office. Once he finally got there, just after taking a morning office break and just before his lunch hour (and a half), he sat down to work on reports and other paperwork. Yes, he was behind but he also had to volunteer applications and read updates from the Association. Volunteers had to be ever so carefully screened so as to not allow potentially dangerous persons (like certain members of First Church, just kidding, shame on you, Al). No, really, the Association was more concerned with former convicts and the mentally unstable (their words).

Al didn't return to the office. He couldn't help but feel like he'd done what he needed to do today. He went to lunch and then to the lake. He stood in for someone as they handled an equipment issue, blow up balloons. He assisted with some games and was asked to tell the story. He stayed until the end of the whole thing. He had a lot of fun. He began to understand Carol's affection for these Bible clubs. He watched over as the team dispensed along with the participants. Out by the lake, just like our Lord. He even thought about walking on water, if only… No walking on water but there were flat rocks at his feet. He picked up a few and skipped them as far as he could.

Oh, look, lunch time, almost but close enough. Nobody would say anything if he went to lunch early. He was the boss, after all. That is, unless some big wig from the Association showed up just minutes before his lunch break. They have been known to do that from time to time. But he didn't care anymore. And, sometimes some church leader would come in and try to tell him their opinion of early, long breaks. He *really* didn't care about their opinion. They *really* should mind their own.

But then, oh how much he wanted to go out to the lake after lunch. The Bible clubs began at just around 1:00. It's okay, though, he'd be out there all day tomorrow and the next, and then on Friday and Saturday. If only he could go out there on Sunday as well. Hey what about this, if he preached to them on Saturday *and* invited them to his church on Sunday? That could work. He did have to be here on Sunday because they were still sporadic about the music ministers. Why not just utilize the college for that? He could put that idea in motion.

Oh, man, 3:00, he'd been at this for two hours, just about. He'd been at his desk now for this whole time doing work, the work that was actually expected of him. So, he rose up from his desk and broke for the kitchen where there would be coffee, for a break, of sorts. His eyes strained from staring at a computer screen. He even managed to pull a muscle in his neck in an unsuccessful (still seated) attempt at retrieving a file.

He walked around until just about 4:30. Then he just went home. He'd had enough for the day, all the while in envy of those on the lake today. Oh, how much promise in tomorrow. He considered his Bermuda…style shorts and his Hawaiian (from somewhere other than) shirt. He'll retrieve his beat up old sandals and just make a day of it. Yeah, it would be fun and *they* wouldn't find him out there.

"Where were you?" they would ask.

"Why, I was about my Father's business," he would reply.

Yeah, that would work well. No, not really. If one is not there where they wanted one to be, well…

He went straight home. He drank a can of soda, ate some sugary snack, and excited himself over what to wear the next day and the day after. He hadn't experienced this much control over his own life in a while. He was so excited about his shorts. But, would they still fit? Now, Al, what kind of a woman are you? You're not! Don't act like one… Will these shorts fit? He wore them last year, a year ago.

How many pounds ago? If he tried them on, he would be a woman. But, if he didn't, he might be in for a big surprise tomorrow.

They fit! He stayed up late in jubilation. He almost called one of the guys, but…they just wouldn't understand. What was he saying?! Now, let's see, what sort of television program or food in his fridge would rescue his manhood just now? But, oh those shows for men are chock full of the very influences he did not need right now. You know what the worst part was? He actually snuck a peek at his backside in the mirror. He was such a woman, but just for today. Tomorrow, he would be…a kid, out here on the lake. Will Bob and Alice be there? He certainly hoped their children would be.

He stayed up too late. Then he woke up too early. But the first thing he thought of in the morning were the shorts. Why, of all things? Now, Al, take your time. Go over to it and read your daily devotional. Forget the shorts. Oh, no, is it raining? Thankfully, it wasn't. Instead, it was so sunshiny. He sat in front of his window to do his reading. He basked in the warmth of the sun. Then he proceeded to meditate on the Word of God. He listened to God through His Word and through nature. But, boy, was he tired. He could hardly wait for his coffee.

What songs would they sing today? They were always fun songs. Before he knew it, he was sporting those shorts. Keys, must place keys in pocket. If he were to lock himself out of the house and could not drive his car because his keys were locked inside the house, his day would be shot to…there, that place. And, what about his wallet? It should would come in handy when he stopped at the store for coffee on the way. Coffee and donuts, enough for everybody? Team of four, how many donuts is that? How much coffee is that? What if there were nondrinkers of the stuff on the team? For that matter, what if some did not eat donuts? Who doesn't eat donuts?

He showed up at the lake with a dozen donuts and a box of coffee. Two of them had a big look on their faces, not just for the breakfast but to see him there. They hugged his neck and greeted him. He expressed his excitement at this opportunity and thought maybe he had arrived overdressed. They all looked so ragged. And that third person, a guy with a whistle around his neck. He looked like a PE coach. He may very well have been. He was here to lead the games. His part would be first. A real nice lady would then lead the songs.

At 11:30, he decided to go to Alice's and offer them a ride out there. He thought that may just be what they needed from him. Meet them where they're at. That's what Jesus would do. But, would he have a van? Wait, the team had arrived here In a van. And it belonged to the mission. So, he left his car keys with the team members, in case they needed it for anything. And he drove the van out to get Alice and the kids. He hadn't driven it in quite a while. But he was still excited to do this. Wow, driving the 15 passenger van out to pick up people for church, well...

And it turned out to be a good idea. She got the kids ready, brought out the car seat, and instructed her kids to be good at church, uh, the Bible club. She came along as well because she was concerned about their behavior and because the little one wanted to go with brother and sister (or 'bruver and sisser as he said it). Al didn't have an issue with it. But, would there be anyone else? As a matter of fact, there was. Remember Aaron Wilson? He had been spending a lot of time with this family. The kids loved him. And he never felt so wanted.

He was a little old for the Bible clubs, but it was doable. And he would be a great help He was an awkward kid. But he was loved by everyone. He also came out with excessive energy. That proved an important trait in keeping up with these kids. There was, of course, the fact that going out there meant seeing that spot in the lake. So, gave him a heads up. He didn't mind. He's not scared anymore. And, besides, Ms Alice said Bobby was in heaven and that's a better place. The little one kept reaching a hand out to him from the confines of his car seat. Everybody was okay again.

Aaron seemed to really enjoy the games they played. He helped to direct the younger children. He also carried his little buddy throughout it all. Alice's two older ones had a really great time. Al even joined in on the fun. The kids all laughed when ever he lost his balance and took a tumble. He didn't mind, though. And the coach did a fine job of directing traffic. Kids at play was kids at work. Laughter filled the area. It was for all intensive purposes, Biblical Joy.

The song leader led the kids in a few songs complete with the motions. Little one sat in Aaron's lap, singing and clapping. Her little girl sang like a canary. Her son didn't seem to want to sing, but he joined in anyway. Other people in the area were watching and pointing. A few kids came over from their campsites.

'The more, the merrier', Al thought.

He didn't think for a moment about what he was missing back at the mission. He was about his Father's business out there. And, he would be at it again tomorrow as well. He may never go back. This is what it's all about.

His thoughts were interrupted by the lady leading the singing. She had instructed everyone to sit at the onset of the last song.

"It's time for the story," she announced.

"Oh, yes, so it is," Al responded.

He began by looking up into the sky. Some of the kids looked too but nobody knew why.

"I'm going to tell the story of Noah's ark. But, first, I wanted to see if it's going to rain, maybe even for forty days and nights."

The kids, and adults, giggled.

"If it does, we're going to have to get busy and build an ark, a houseboat, or something. But, as long as it doesn't rain, we can go ahead with the story.

A second later, the little one moved from Aaron's lap to his. He smiled and continued.

"You see, the world was going crazy. All the people, except Noah and his family, were being bad."

A little girl asked, "What were they doing?"

"Some very bad things," he replied, patiently.

"Did they break their sister's doll?" she inquired as she looked over at a boy who might have been her brother.

"Uh, yes, but anyway, Noah…"

Maybe not.

"Did they lie to their mommy?"

"Yes, and God told Noah to build an ark because they had been so bad. Her eyes got big.

"He told Noah there was going to be a flood.

She looked at the sky.

"He said to load not only his family but two of every kind of animal onto the ark.

She was his biggest fan.

"So, Noah Noah built the ark and obeyed God, even though the bad people made fun of him."

"What did they say?" she asked just as he thought her questions were over.

"They made fun of him because he said it was going to rain.

Nothing, she just stared at him. He thought it best to continue while he can.

"He finished the ark and loaded his family…"

"…and the animals," someone else's child said.

"Yes, and the animals, two by two…"

"Why?" she chimed in again.

"Why what?" he asked.

"two by two…" she inquisoned.

Oh, no, not a lesson on reproduction. But another adult rang the bell that saved the day.

"How about we allow Mr. Bryant to finish the story?"

It was Alice. He nodded his appreciation and she smiled.

"After the ark was loaded, the rains came down…

He expected someone, almost anyone, to sing the song 'and the floods came up', but no one did.

"And it flooded after 40 days and forty nights of rain. Then Noah stayed on the ark for about four whole months."

"Then what happened?" another child, one of Alice's, asked.

"The waters dried up."

He then fielded questions like ground balls. They wanted to know what happened after that, when Jesus came, about the dove and the stick, and other very interesting questions. He even learned a few things. Then Alice assisted the craft leader work with the kids on arks made with thoroughly-washed out milk cartons. Then the parents came and retrieved them and the day was over.

Al was too tuckered to not go home. On the way, he exited the highway at exit 114 and went through a drive-through for tacos. He reentered the highway and could think about nothing but the huge blessing he had just received. Even the inquisitive ones were such a joy. He laughed as he thought about it. He laughed, smiled, and sang all the way home.

"The rains came down and the floods came up.

The rains came down and the floods came up."

7

TV and crosswords used up his evening. A shower and a nice time thanking God for his wonderful day soon followed. He hadn't felt so useful in so long. He thought about how he had spent the whole day away from the office. Something about middle-age makes one feel so responsible for all things expected of you. Oh, well... He also prayed so hard for those kids and their families. Finally, he begged for some definition of his true calling, admin or missionary. He felt like an evangelist right about now. He couldn't wait until tomorrow.

On Wednesday, he woke up to rain. Oh, no, this is unbelievable. Would he cancel, should he? After all, he was the boss. He could cancel and go back to the mission for the day. But that would prove depressing. And he just knew that someone from the Association would call if he did. He found himself playing the avoidance game. *What do you mean 'like he did yesterday?'* He was avoiding responsibility. He was avoiding the Association and the churches as well. He was avoiding some of the volunteers, but more than that the people in need of him. He was having too much fun.

Yet, he would have to at least check in at his office before going out there. He had to make sure everything would be set up for the Wednesday evening meal and service. But, once lunch time arrived, he would be so...gone...from there. He would officially be...out... the door. But, what about the rain? He wanted to go out there no matter what. Then he remembered the shelter that was out there. But, would the parents bring the children if it rained? And, what of the ones who did? The team would have to be there just in case, or, at least, someone would be.

He left for the lake after an early lunch. So far, nothing had gone his way. They weren't ready for anybody in the lunchroom. He had to wait. He forgot his keys when he first went out the door. He almost turned the wrong direction… coming out of the parking lot. And people looked at him strangely when he left. It was like 'how dare he'. It began to rain again along the way. 'Bring on the rain'. What was he saying? Why was he already experiencing disappointment? Was he going the right direction?

The team had gone out to pick up Alice and crew but little one was sick and the other two were preoccupied. Nothing was said in regards to Aaron. They just did not possess the rapport he did with these people. Coordination and organization as well stayed home that day. There was even dissention in the ranks. The coach forgot the parachute, which wouldn't have been useful in the rain anyway. Hey, by the way, what sort of games could they play in the shelter? Uh, well, there won't be that many kids there today anyway. What to do?

It rained off and on. So, they utilized the shelter. And, wouldn't you know it? Some kids showed up who would just happen to be the last kids you would want to have shown up if you were forced to be indoors. These particular kids were closterphobic, hyper active, un(der)disciplined, and just downright mean, both of them. That's right, there were two of them, twin boys. The problem was the two-way instigation with no means of separation. Their parents also showed no interest in controlling them.

The time came upon them for Al to teach about David and Goliath. He thought the interruptions were bad the day before. Today, it was really bad because the interruptions were not the product of innocent curiosity but a distaste for his teaching material, the Bible. Their parents said they didn't care for the story because it taught violence and they *"simply abhorred violence"*. The irony of all that was that the boys kept fighting each other while bullying smaller children who had showed up later. As a matter of fact, they always seemed to be on their absolute worst behavior whenever mom was enthralled in conversation.

They made crowns of cardboard and paper plates because David would become king. This mother complained about it because she felt as though they were being cheap with materials. They were never entirely certain about dad's feelings because it didn't seem like he had even been allowed an opinion. Oh, well, you probably didn't want to hear it anyway, his opinion, that is. Mom complained about the little (fake) gems they put on their crown. Did she expect real ones? Yeah, you're right, she probably did.

The whole day had been a disaster. He was certain that whole family would return to wherever it was they had come from and tell everyone all about it. Would that ruin the team, the whole ministry for next year? Where had they come from anyway? Were they locals? (I swear I didn't say 'locos') or were they from abroad? Their car pulling away was a pleasant sight and sound, the best he'd had all day. Thinking about the four of them had him feeling sorry for... who? They deserved each other and the parents were reaping what they'd sown. He chuckled at that thought. He could picture the boys driving mom crazy while she nagged dad.

Al went back to the mission. He thought he'd eat dinner there and hang around for his usual Wednesday evening teaching. He was teaching out of the Epistles of the Apostles. As usual, more would come for the free dinner than would stay for the teaching. Well, they were there to serve, after all. But, they were also there to teach, evangelize, and baptize. And with the way his day had gone, He wasn't certain who would listen anyway. What would those who did listen think and would they actually listen?

He guesstimated that there were about 100 at dinner. He'd love to teach one hundred people that evening that they are not saved by works, but by grace. Dinner wasn't really that much that night, just some soup and sandwiches. Given his day, that was to be expected. The food was made cheap and somehow managed to cost even less. Also, no Bob and Alice as he had hoped. There were a few regulars but no one from the Bible clubs. Oh, no, this simply would not do, at all. Well, sit and eat. That much he could do. The soup was cold and the sandwich colder. He needed energy for this evening. He simply wasn't motivated.

He was right. About half stayed for the teaching.

"Where two or more are gathered…there am I", Jesus had said.*

They shuffled in after a long while of fellowship and gossip in the hallway. They still conversed as they sat in their seats. It was almost like he wasn't even there. He figured on allowing for more conversation consisting in approximately an hour's worth. That would certainly teach them.

But, no, he was their leader, so…

"Welcome, everyone to the Wednesday night Bible study."

Some peered up to him as if to say, "Are you absolutely certain it's your turn to talk? We're not quite finished." He continued, not feeling it at all, "I'm glad you're all here.

*scripture quoted from Matthew 18:20 (NLT)

'What, really?'

"Are there any praise reports tonight?"

A hand went up.

"Yes?" he managed.

It was a little old lady he and Carol had visited before.

"Preacher, I thank God for all my pets. They're all I got."

"That's great, *anyone* else?"

A few gave thanks but not many seemed grateful for anything.

After a moment of silent prayer, he accepted prayer requests. Oh, here we go, fodder for gossip. People would take some of this out of here and spread it all around the area to those who did not attend (including those who would never attend). He had wanted in times past to just have them write them down and he would do the praying for these requests at a later time. But, no, he probably wouldn't have time. So, they shared and prayed. Then a young man from the college led the singing. It seemed as though he were accustomed to a much younger crowd because his music seemed to take off without them. He, therefore, did most of the singing himself. The lady with the pets smiled up at him. And the lady from a while back at the Valentine's banquet announcement smiled at Al. Oh, no!

"Tonight", he began his teaching, if for no other reason than to get it over with. "We go over the Epistles of the Apostles.

He felt as though he were pushing a train up a hill (one of those two engine ones.)

"These Epistles begin at Romans, where we were before in our discussion regarding salvation. Then are the Corinthians, followed by Galatians, Ephesians, Philippians, and Colossians. Several smaller Epistles follow, including some by both Peter and John."

He taught about people getting drunk in Corinth at the Lord's Supper. He taught the truth that we reap what we sew and the works of the flesh as well as the fruits of the Spirit. He then spoke of husbands, wives, and the Gospel Armor. There were good points in both Philippians and Colossians as well. He told about the story of Philemon. He bounced right into and out of the idea that no one is certain of the authorship of the book of Hebrews. He said he believed that James (who wrote the book of James) was the brother of Jesus, as was Jude. When he spoke of John's letters and how they spoke of love, he looked out over his audience and saw none of it.

On Thursday, he came into the office. He had some catching up to do. The team of volunteers handled the Bible Club. He had no idea as to who would be there. He had hopes, though. There could be no doubt about it, his body may be at the mission but his mind (and his heart) Would be out on that lake. He just hoped he could concentrate on his reports, not that anyone from the Association would interrupt him anyway. He wondered if it worked the other way as well. If he *wanted* one of them to call, he could begin filling out a report...

Sure enough, he got a call.

"Al Bryant here."

"Al, this is Dennis from the university."

Oops, guessed wrong.

"What can I do for you?"

"Al, I'm just calling to let you know I've got a couple of guys going out to the Lake on Sunday to do the chapel service."

He still really wanted to do that himself.

"Uh," Al began, "I was just wondering about one of them becoming my permanent music guy here at the mission."

"You don't have anyone?"

"Music ministers from the Association churches have been coming out on Sundays. But I just don't feel alright about taking them from their duties at their churches."

"Yeah, Al, we've been sending young people out to those churches weekly. I guess we could cut out the middle man. But, some of the students seem to enjoy serving in churches because that's what they're working towards."

"All I want is one. The others can just go out to their churches."

That's when he thought about why these music ministers had wanted to serve at the mission when those students served at their churches. It just didn't feel right to be there when the young people were doing *their* job. And it would also be weird for the congregation. And the students could use the exposure as well. But he felt the need, the urge to obtain just one.

"Can we do that?" he continued.

Dennis said he would coverse with the one who was scheduled to lead the singing on Sunday. Al accepted that and carried on his duties. He wrote a report on the Bible clubs. But he couldn't find any place on the whole form to write about the cute little questioner or about Aaron's contribution. And, what about the family from yesterday? Did they ever want to know that there were some who didn't like it at all? All they wanted were numbers. Those numbers justified money allotted to the mission.

The next day he wasted no time getting ready to go out there. But he remembered Wednesday and decided to take some time to pray first. He read scripture out of the gospels. Then he played some old Christian music from days past. While listening, he thanked God for a better day, new opportunities. He confessed fear and doubt stemming from what he considered a fiasco on Wednesday. He proceeded to pray for Alice, her kids, and Aaron. He also lifted up all who would be there today. He hoped for the questioner but hoped against the troubles (but he immediately repented and gulped down a prayer for himself.)

He laid his whole self down before God in surrender of all that God would do through him on that day. He presented himself an empty jar of clay, broken and spilled out. He actually looked forward to seeing what God would do today.

"Just follow the Spirit," he reminded himself as he thought about Alice, the kids, Aaron, and Bob.

What these kids took from here would go on to affect their parents meaningfully and assuredly.

He arrived, no Alice and the kids, so he once again exchanged his keys for the keys of the van. Then he proceeded on this wonderful Friday...to take a leisurely drive in their general direction. No highway this time, state road instead. Lots of old relics (people, places, and things) to see along the way. There may be cows, tractors, maybe even some deer along the way, right out on the road. Amish buggies were another possibility. Just remember, don't drive into the smoke, especially in that Association van. Would he stop along the way? He hadn't had lunch and hardly had breakfast. But, what about his passengers?

For that reason, he stopped in a little store and got a dozen donuts. He also got a fill-up of coffee. But then he realized the gas tank read a quarter full on the gauge. They were supposed to fill it up the day before. Were they aware he'd be using the van today? Oh, yeah, he was the mission director. After all is said and done, this type of thing fell on his shoulders. That's alright. A leisurely drive requires a fill-up on gas. He spoke with the old guy behind the counter for twenty minutes before proceeding on his journey.

He purposely left the donuts in the seat behind him so the kids would be pleasantly surprised by these sweets. He hoped mom would allow them the indulgence, just for today. It was his gift. Alice came out carrying Little One on her hip. The two older ones raced out to the van. He thought she beat him. James accused Lindsey of cheating because there could be no way she could've beat him any other way. The side door on the van came open and James saw the box on the seat. But he didn't say or do anything. His folks had taught him well.

After everyone was all in, Al asked if anyone wanted a donut. They looked at mom. She had fed them breakfast already, so she okayed this little extra. Her little one, Peter, reached out a hand for a donut. She got one for him and they shared it. The other two each took one and Al grabbed one for the road. He felt elated as they all thanked him. He was ever so glad to share that wonderful confection with such a sweet family. It was also a wonderful blessing to watch the little one go at it with such vigor.

Aaron was surprised to see him. Alice had gotten out of the van and taken Peter with her to the door of his home to inquire of his parents as to whether or not he could accompany them. Al had reminded Alice to mention the cook-out that is to take place tomorrow for all the families. He knew he'd have to remember to remind people today about it. But, what about this little family's lunch today? That's when he noticed the small basket sitting on the seat. She had, apparently brought it out in the free hand. Now, what about his lunch? E didn't care. He was excited about today, tomorrow, even Sunday.

Aaron climbed into the van. Al offered him a donut. He took it. He ate it, too. The other two asked for another. Al left that up to mom, who said yes. Even she accepted another. All the donuts were gone by the time they arrived at the lake. He took the long way back to the lake. Everyone remarked on the country side. Peter fell asleep. He thought that James and Lindsey might also, but not Aaron.

He thought about it for a second, than he asked Alice,

"Do you think Bob will come out tomorrow?"

"I think so," she answered with a sigh.

"Is something wrong?"

"No, it's just that there's a job he's been working on that he hopes he'll get finished today."

"Oh, well, I hope so. I'd like to see him."

"Me, too."

They arrived about an hour before the Bible club was scheduled to begin. Alice took the kids over to a park bench and spread out their lunch.

'Oh, no,' Al thought, "what about the donuts?'

It didn't seem to phase those little balls of energy to share their lunch with Aaron. She offered some to Al but he respectfully declined and walked over to the concession stand.

Unfortunately, though, he had to do something else first. It was something that would require him to use the facilities. He wasn't too happy about it but it had to be done. These things were nasty, smelly, full of who knows what types of bacteria? And, on a few occasions, some patrons were known to mistake it for a hotel room. The writing on the wall was none too flattering, either. He hoped to see no one else in there. He was nervous about that the whole time. But, what if someone did come in and needed Jesus? The gospel might save this place. The gospel could save this whole lake.

No one came in and he was almost disappointed (not because he was looking for a good time but because he wanted to preach the gospel to someone.) He had wanted to see them receive an sterna good time in heaven. Oh, well, where's that concession stand with the burgers, dogs, fries, pops, and heartburn? It was to his left. So, he made a bee line for it. Oh, man, what a mistake. What if he got chili on his dog and reacted to it while telling the story? No chili? Who ever heard of such a thing?

After lunch, he headed back to the site. As he drew closer, he noticed several families going that way. Wow, there were a lot of kids going to be there today. He got nervous. C'mon, he preached to and taught this many people pretty regularly at the mission. But, they weren't people. They were children. What would he do with twenty-five inquisitions and twenty-five troubles?

'Stop, turn around, run!'

'No, don't do that! This is exactly what you came for.'

Six sets of parents as well made a promising turnout for Saturday.

'Oh, wait, run down there as fast as you can to remind everyone'

Will the team do that?

He got down there and the coach got the games started almost immediately. But first he had to explain the directions and rules of the game. It would require lots of energy. It would involve loads of fun. And it would, very possibly, lead to laughter. Aaron was the hero to all the kids in this and the following games. He made the balls bounce high off the parachute. And he was so fast they couldn't catch him in freeze tag. Well, a few of the smaller ones managed, somehow (wink, wink) to catch him, somehow. It was fun just to watch.

The song leader, of course, led everyone in a rousing rendition of Zachaeus. Even Peter learned the motions for the song. When they sang "Zaccheus was a wee little man"*

He put his hand close to the ground as an indication of his smallness. And he made the climbing motions as well. Alice showed him how. He received a lot of attention on this one. All eyes were on him. As they sang the song about a man in the Bible* who had been short of stature and the lord told him to come out of the tree, he shook his finger. A few more songs and it would be Al's turn to tell the story. He got an inspiration, though. He would ask Alice's permission to use her son to help with the story. It was such a cute idea, he didn't stop smiling.

Al sat the kids around him and informed them he was going to tell the story of *Zaccheus. But, he announced he had a little helper for this one. He looked toward Alice and she handed over her little one, who gladly went to Al. After sitting in the lap Al made (obviously for him) he looked up at him as if to say,

"What we going to do?"

But he didn't really say anything. The trust in his little eyes was truly inspiring. So, Al began with the story.

He said, as he looked down at Petey,

*"You see, *Zaccheus was indeed a wee little man."

"Like Petey," someone offered.

8

"Not quite as small as this little one but you get the idea. Anyway,* Jesus was walking down the street. He had quite a few people with Him."

"Why?"

It was her. She was back! That's great!

"He was...popular.

She must have known what that meant because she didn't inquire.

"You see,* Zaccheus was a tax collector."

"What's...a...tas...coleter?"

"A *tax collector* is someone who takes money from people...but not stealing."

Peter looked at him without his usual smile.

A little boy looked sad and shot his hand up.

A question from someone other than...?

"Yes?"

"Daddy says taxes are why we don't have a house anymore."

"Then, I think you'll like this story.

At this point, he lifted Peter up.

*"Zachaeus wasn't tall enough to see Jesus. So, he climbed a tree.

He knew better than to mention it was a Sycamore tree, because he couldn't answer that question. He lifted Peter up like was climbing a tree.

IDEA

He got Aaron to be the tree and Petey climbed him. Aaron held him up for the rest of the story.

"*Jesus walked up and looked up into the tree.

He instructed all of the kids to wag their fingers at Petey, uh, Zaccheus. He thought it was funny, as did his mommy.

"He said, everybody now...

And altogether, they sang the end of the song.

He motioned for Aaron to put Petey back down. He stood and clapped his little hands, for himself.

Everyone clapped for him, and Aaron. Alice placed Petey in her lap and Aaron sat next to Al. Al looked at the boy from before and continued,

"*Jesus went to Zaccheus' house. He was so glad to have Jesus at his house. This is the part you might like. He promised to repay all of the tax money.

*Luke19 (NLT)

He smiled at that.

"Jesus can change any of us."

They all drew trees for the craft.

Al spoke with the boy. He found out that the government made his family move out of their house because they didn't have any money. They were having to stay at his grandma's and mom and dad are trying to get another house. He said that he missed his room and his yard and all of his friends. And now he has to go to a different school. He said the government guys were real mean and made them pack the boxes and put them in the truck. And, according to his sad little self, his mom and dad argue all the time now.

"We used to be so happy."

His parents came to get him. His grandparents as well. Al made a point of meeting them. He hoped he could help them at the mission. Man, that would give him a reason to come to work on Monday. And, he needed to be sure to invite them out for Saturday's festivities. What if they didn't come Saturday, tomorrow? I know, give card today and tomorrow, if they need it tomorrow. He couldn't allow them to go out of here without offering to help.

Well, here goes.

He grabbed the right hand of the dad and shook it.

"Al", he introduced.

"Joe", he replied, "nice to meet you. Thanks for inviting Kevin."

"Thanks for bringing him."

"Dad", Kevin interrupted, "guess what, Jesus is going to get our tax money back."

Dad laughed.

Al said, "I, uh, told a Bible story today that talked about that."

"Zachaeus?" Joe inquired.

"Uh, yes."

"I remember hearing that story when I was a kid. Isn't there a song?"

Yes, there is. The song kind of tells the story. Anyway, I would like to take this opportunity to extend an invitation to all of you for the cook-out tomorrow, right here."

The couple looked at each other. They seemed uncertain.

"I'm Sandy, Kevin's mom. Thank you for the invite, but I don't know."

"Well," Al continued, "don't decide yet. It all begins about three o'clock tomorrow, right here. Notice, I said 'about three', so don't worry about being late. We'll be here until six or seven.

He pulled out a card.

"Here's my card. Oh, and we'll be out here on Sunday as well to hold a chapel service at eleven a.m. And, if you ever need anything, my number and the address of our mission are right there."

Halfway home, he had to do a head count. That's when he remembered that Alice and the kids were taken home by the team.

He had been day dreaming about that family. This was the reason he had wanted to work in this field in the first place. That little boy, kevin's story had touched him in a profound way. He hoped to see the family tomorrow and hear from Joe and Sandy. He also wondered what the grandparent's take was after having their home invaded by this family. Invaded, really?

He didn't go back to work. He would allow the volunteers to pick up the supplies in the morning. Carol would never have done something like that. She would return to the mission and wait until the details were realized. And then volunteers would know of her plans so they would just go home. Then they would complain tomorrow because she was running late. No, not this lone missionary. He would put his thing down tonight at the bowling alley with his friends, his unchurched, raw, unsophisticated (religiously, anyway), crude, rude dudes. That what he was going to be tonight.

He bowled with his friends. But all he could think about was Bob and Joe. He had hoped Bob would be at the cook-out. He also wanted Joe to want his help. You'd think they were his brothers the way he seemed to feel about each of them. And, what about these guys here tonight? They were like brothers as well. The sense of brotherhood surrounded him. He thought of Jesus in the midst of them.

What was a mission-minded man? The center of mission work is the work of Christ. The idea is to plant and water. Plant the seed and cultivate it. He was cultivating now. But it's work. Work and do the job Jesus set us forth to do. Baptize and teach. Disciple and pray. Be witnesses of Him throughout the land and the world. Know Him and make Him known. Go forth the land and the world, sharing God's love and salvation. The message of salvation is in our fruits and our spirit.

When he got home, he couldn't turn on the tv because it might taint his thoughts. It might not convey his message. Besides, all he wanted was quiet. He sat in his office, thinking, praying, asking God to give him Bob and Joe. He considered those bowling friends of his.

He had never thought about them in this way before. He somehow considered them in the same context as Bob and Joe. He had never before thought of them in the context of his ministry.

He felt at peace, somehow. He rejected peace because he still wanted to be angry about Carol. But, face it, he was over that. They hadn't made up for it. But he was over it. That's not right. He felt as though those feelings betrayed her somehow. He can't possibly go on although he can. His resentment had somehow subsided. No, not yet. He wasn't ready. What was holding him back? Or, was he moving past this just to go on to something else? Whatever that was, he wasn't ready for it. That had to be it, though.

He had a dream about a church. He was the pastor of it. The thing was, though, it consisted only of men. He noticed Bob, Aaron, Joe, Kevin and his grandfather, and all of his bowling buddies. One was missing, though, although it was hard to tell because they were all sitting in the back. He saw the premadonnaman guitar player, the middle-aged video game addict, and a few other guys who had been through the mission. But there were no women and he was happy with that.

Saturday, he went to the mission before going out to the lake. The whole team came there first as well. He thought it best for all concerned if they rode together in the van. He'd prayed for Bob and Joe to show up today. There was no preaching today, no teaching. They'd cook burgers and dogs, pass out chips and pops, and help in whatever way they could. He also prayed Bob and Alice would pick up Aaron along the way. As a matter of fact, he gathered the team for prayer before departing for the site.

They arrived at the site about noon. They immediately set things up. Al got the grill going. Coach insisted on assisting with the charcoaling. Al thought it might be a contest between the two of them for grilling duties. But, Al did want to talk to Joe today. So, he would have to surrender the grill at some point. And coach couldn't leave early without taking their transportation with him. Running the grill was the man's job and here he was bested by his own desire of duty.

People began to show about 1:00 as had been announced. Al watched them arrive one family at a time. His heart sank every time it wasn't Bob and Alice or Joe and Sandy. He was afraid he hadn't emphasized it enough. Either that or they were only humoring him when they said they'd come today. There must have been a hundred other things they'd rather do today. Maybe they just forgot. Both spouses not to mention all of those children, all forgot. Oh, wait, that was the reason. Do you realize the difficulty in organizing all of those adults and children together at the same time on a Saturday?

Just as he was about to give up, he saw…both families arriving right behind each other. Bob and Alice arrived first. Their kids, and Aaron, piled out of the car. Then he saw Kevin get out of the car behind them. Joe got out, followed by Sandy. And then he saw the grandparents. They were all there. Now, he felt guilty for doubting them. More than that, he had doubted God. He went from way down in the lower regions to high above the clouds (except for the guilt).

The adults all saw him and made their way towards him. He shook all of their hands and expressed his sheer delight in having them there. They all talked for a minute. It seems as though Bob had had some car trouble and Joe stopped to help him. Amazing, wasn't it? He was concerned that neither family would come today but they both arrived, together. Al pointed out the grill and the table with all of the fixings. He also came to realize how much these two men had in common as they had both lost house and home in the crash. And there were a lot of others in this area as well.

They talked as they ate. Al gave them the option to either meet at the office or out there tomorrow. He informed them he'd be at the mission but a couple of gifted college volunteers would be out there for the chapel service. Joe said but failed to commit to coming out to the mission. Bob and Alice, however, said they'd like to see those college kids. The grandparents expressed concern for the welfare of the children going to that "mission type place". But Alice assured them it was alright.

The grandparents seemed to be concerned about everything that day. Al wanted to get alone with them just to talk over their concerns. Grandpa didn't say much. Grandma did all the talking. But what she said didn't make a lot of sense. She talked about church and the preacher. Sandy shared she'd wanted to go to church for some time but she just didn't know how to approach it with Joe. Joe had had a bad experience with the church after his parents' divorce. It seemed their church frowned upon such things.

What a week! They'd done such great work, reached so many. They reminded everyone (he hoped) of the upcoming chapel service the following day. There was little mention of church at the mission. But that's because this had been an Associational event. Only one member of the team had mentioned their own church to anyone. What would transpire here? Some of the participants already went to church, somewhere. That included Bob and Alice. Only a few of them might still go unreached. But then there would be the revival and harvest party.

Al had closure this week on a lot of things: Carol, Bobby, and a few others. But he still needed more. He carried around some baggage, for sure. He said good-bye to his team at the mission. He said good-bye to Bobby at the lake. And he said good-bye to Carol. A few more to say, that's all. He was ready, however, to say hello to some sleep. Say good-bye to the week and hello to some rest. Tomorrow would begin a new week. There was promise in that new beginning. He had some serious praying to do.

On Sunday, he sensed the urgency to prophesy of the coming Christ. When he awoke in the morning, his heart was ablaze with the message of salvation, the hope of new life, and the warning of the Spirit. He basked in the severity of the moment. He knew that people all around him had but one last chance to decide on Christ or self. At least he knew this could possibly be their last opportunity to receive Christ. He had to preach this message now before it was too late. He would prophesy this morning of the coming of Christ.

So, he meditated on some scripture from Revelation. It warned of being lukewarm and not hot or cold. It spoke of God spewing them out. He carefully considered what it meant for him and the folks he would be speaking to this morning. What did it say regarding the remainder of his summer? Now that Bible clubs were over, for the mission anyway, would he get stuck in some kind of holding pattern? Is this where he would get lazy? He needed to focus on the words of the Father. He remembered that Jesus said this to John in a dream. What did this mean to *him*?

"The Son of Man will come as a thief in the night, is what he started with.

"Honestly, how many of you would be prepared?

"Jesus told his apostles that some of them would not die before the return of the Son of Man. But all of them did. Who, though, is He really speaking to? The Bible has been around for centuries. I think, I believe He was speaking to us.

"Many of us will not die before His return. But, by us, I'm referring to you, me, and future generations. In other words, not every believer will die before His return We just don't know the hour. And, by His own admission, neither does He. If we had an idea whether the antichrist were alive today, we would then have a time frame of some sort. He might be alive or he hasn't been born yet. But he is the only prophesy yet unfulfilled. There was some indication that Caesar might have been 'the one'. He brought peace to the world. People bowed to him. He was murdered. But he didn't come back to life. Satan will take over the antichrist when he resurrects.

"There are three schools of thought on the return of Christ. Some believe He will return before the millennium, which is the reign of Satan for a thousand years. Anyway, they are what's known as premillennialists. Some others say He will return during, They are the amillennialist. Finally, there are the postmillennialists who believe in His return after it's all over with. Which is the truth?

Study Revelations and figure it out for yourself. I believe He will return first because Satan can't reign in the presence of the Holy Spirit indwelling in these temples (believers).

"If that is indeed the case, we all need to be ready. If He is to return at the beginning of it all, then we need to be ready because we wil not know when to expect Him. And that, indeed, is what Jesus prophesied in the gospels, that we would not be aware of the time of His return, like a thief in the night. How do we prepare? We, as believers, are referred to as the bride of Christ. We, as such, are prepared a bride is prepared for the bride groom. But the groom knows not when his bride is ready. And, according to His own words, He doesn't even know when. Only the Father knows.

"Don't face God in judgment without Jesus. He is our advocate with the Father. To be prepared is to be washed in the blood of Christ. But it's not a decision to be made lightly. If you choose Christ only half-heartedly, without belief and confession as it says in Romans 10:9&10, you'll live the rest of your life with a false sense of security. So, don't listen to anyone who counts beans when it comes to your decision to follow Christ."

That last remark was a shot at the Association and all of their number crunching. But he really felt like preaching the gospel to sell fire insurance or rack up the numbers in an effort to justify money spent for ministry was sending a false message and inadvertently sending people to hell. If people walk around thinking they are saved when they are not they will be under the illusion of eternal life but instead will find death at the throne of God. Oh, how many false prophets there are in our own denomination.

Al sat at his desk on Monday morning, reading, writing, and making decisions, thinking, dreaming, just really not there in his mind. But a knock at his door landed his dream cloud back at his desk. His eyes went to the door and there he saw Joe, Sandy, and Sandy's mother. He remembered the day before when the two of them, along with Kevin came forward to receive Christ. Grandma almost got up too but Al noticed the look in Grandpa's eyes that managed to sit her back down. That had concerned him.

He stood to greet them, "Joe, Sandy, come on in."

They came in and sat down. Grandma introduced herself.

"Yes", Al replied, "I remember, from the lake, welcome."

"Thank you," Grandma said as she sat down. She appeared to not approve of this visit.

Should he ask? Should he inquire as to the reason why she hadn't come forward?

"So," Al went on, "what brings you here?"

Joe and Sandy looked at each other, kind of puzzled.

Joe answered, "What we talked about yesterday..."

"Yes," Al answered, "but, what exactly do you need from me? How can we work together?"

"Oh, dear." Grandma chimed in.

"Pardon me?" Al inquisoned.

"Oh, nothing. I just thought we were here to get help, not to provide it. My husband and I can work with them."

"Yes, I'm certain you can. But I Would like to help out in any way that I can."

"We're basically looking to move out, find a place of our own," Joe offered.

"We can assist with rent, moving, utilities, perhaps if we make a list of exactly what you need."

He turned to his computer and brought up an empty (blank) document. He was excited to start a file on them.

Grandma spoke up, "I just don't understand all the rush in moving out."

Sandy's turn, "Mom, we've discussed this..."

Then Joe, "We need to have a place of our own."

"Well, excuse me if my home isn't good enough for you," Grandma blurted out.

"Mom, please..." Sandy was flustered.

Al thought about it for a minute and then he offered some advice.

"Folks," he began, "I can see several different emotions at work here. Mom, you want to take care of your child because you know she needs you right now. Joe, you feel like you need to make your way. I get that, I do. And, Sandy, you're caught in the middle."

She nodded in agreement.

"You want your parents to know they are appreciated. But, at the same time, you want to honor your husband."

Grandma again, "I just don't want to see them buying again on loan. I want to see them save their money until they can buy in cash. That's all."

Joe replied, "It's not that simple."

"So, you'd rather pay a bank ridiculous interest rates on an over inflated loan?"

"Mom, it's just the way things are today." That was Sandy.

"You know you can stay with us as long...(gulp) as you...need to." Guess who.

"You hesitated," Joe threw in.

"Yes, I heard it too," Al thoughtlessly added. He knew better than to get in the middle of something like this. Oh, no, he was counseling. Help! Get me out of this!

Grandma looked at him, daggers.

"Yes, Lillian, you hesitated. You don't like us staying with you at all, much less indefinitely.

The computer was still running.

"Besides, what makes you think we're going right out to buy?"

"Oh, so you're going to rent, pay someone else for the rest of your lives and never own?" Lillian was set this time.

"Lillian," Al did it again, "if I may call you that?"

"Yes, Mr.Bryant, that's fine."

"Al, please. Lillian, you're setting up an impossible situation for them. You don't want them to buy. You don't want them to rent. What's it going to be?"

She just sat with her arms crossed.

Sandy's vessel rolled into port, "Mom, we appreciate everything you've done, really. But I agree with Joe that we need to be on our own."

It got quiet, deafly quiet. Al looked at his computer screen. He really wanted to do some work. He didn't want to argue anymore. Besides, it appeared as though everyone was talked out.

"Let's get started here. What do you see as your needs at the moment?" Al started with.

"What do you need to know?" Joe asked.

"For instance, your family size, three?"

Once again, that look toward each other.

"Four," Sandy answered.

"Who is the other?"

Joe spoke up, "My daughter from my first marriage, Christine."

"No problem, four."

"She don't care about nothing or nobody." Grandma.

"Sorry?"

Sandy gave her mom a look of 'please, mom'.

Then she said, "She's sixteen and she's just started driving. We almost never see her anymore."

"Almost?" Al asked. 'Here we go again.' He thought.

"She stays gone."

Joe looked to be on the defensive, doting father, feelings of guilt?

"Kids can be that way when they first start driving." He said.

"She's got her own car," Sandy actually seemed angry, resentful.

"Yeah, your dad…" Joe came back.

Al interjected as he typed, "four, three bedrooms?"

"Yeah."

"Rent or buy, a preference?"

Quiet, real quiet.

Finally, "No," Sandy replied, "no preference."

He finished the housing profile with other questions. As it happened, they ended up working through lunch.

He offered them lunch in the cafeteria. They continued to talk throughout the day. He could tell this wasn't a quiet household, with the possible exception of the apparently uninvolved grandpa and the missing teenager. Probably, Kevin didn't add anything either. But these three, just by the fact that they came in together today. He did manage to finish their wish list. Man, he did some ministry today. He felt as though he could retire now. This was what he was called to do.

They took up his whole day but he definitely didn't mind. He would gladly invest time and effort in this clan. He went home, ate dinner, and watched baseball. Oh, yes, the boys of summer would provide the entertainment this evening. As you have probably guessed by that, he was a baseball fan. It was just about the only thing he and Carol had enjoyed together. They liked opposing teams, but they but they had that in common. As he sat in his chair, watching men half his age making millions of dollars throwing a ball around, He thought of Joe, Sandy, Lillian, and all he could do for them.

He went out visiting on Tuesday. He went to all the people who had come out for the Bible clubs. Many of them were at the clubs this week with one of the other churches. But most of them weren't. He invited them to the Bible study at the mission on Wednesday and to church on Sunday. They acted as though no one else had come to see them all summer. He thought that was kind of sad, really. He went ahead and invited them out to the mission for Wednesday Bible study. It seemed underhanded but he didn't want to lose them for the Kingdom.

He spent the rest of the summer promoting the big fall events, the fall revival and the harvest party. Some had that 'Well, what about Halloween?' look on their face. Okay, so maybe he just imagined that look. But, didn't anyone at all believe in celebrating the harvest of crops the farmers would bring in? No, but they should. And, what about All Saint's Day? It was always such a battle with the Association. All the churches around would have Halloween parties and all of the kids would dress like monsters and other demonic beings. But not at his party.

The first Sunday in September, he walked into the chapel. He now had a regular music leader. The song leader from the summer chapel services had agreed to come to work at the mission on Sundays. He no longer needed to worry from week to week about the music. And the numbers in his services had increased since his follow-up visitation. He felt a little guilty about that because he thought he had stolen some prospects from the churches. "Snooze you lose" he guessed it was, though. And there was also Joe, Sandy, and family.

He approached the podium and a hush fell among the people. He looked around at all of the faces. They had changed from the old crowd. Some college kids had started coming in to support the new music guy, Donnie. Others were from the Bible clubs. Some he could remember clear back from the spring food drives and clothing closet. He saw Bob and Alice. They had Aaron with them. His parents still weren't coming out, though. Joe's daughter came once and he hoped to see her again. Lillian decided against him because they had not solved all of Joe and Sandy's problems as she had expected.

He began, as usual, with announcements.

"Good morning, everyone. As usual, it's good to see all of you. I hope you're all doing well. I just wanted to remind all of those involved of the recovery meeting tonight. Oh, before I forget, I just want to welcome friends of Donnie's here this morning. Let me remind everyone of the annual revival in two weeks and the Harvest party in October. That's all just before we start our holiday celebrations."

As usual, a volunteer had been asked to read the scripture reading for the message. He had chosen a passage from Joshua one to preach out of today. Then Donnie led in some singing. It seemed like a more energetic crowd than from before. Another volunteer prayed after requests for thanksgiving were taken. That was followed by communion and prayer request cards were collected. Al said a silent prayer in request of direction for this ever so diverse congregation he faced today. How could he reach all of these people at once? Donnie had been bringing in a soloist every week for special music. And then they handed it over to Al.

"Today, I come out of Joshua chapter one. In this passage, God calls Joshua to commit his life to Him. Joshua chooses God and then calls on a nation to do the same. The people of Israel had time and again chosen other false gods. If you choose not to believe in God, someday you will believe. But that day will arrive too late. When you are brought face to face with your creator, it will be too late to choose, too late to believe. So, choose you this day whom you will serve."

He gave the invitation and several stepped forward. One of those was Aaron. But it was like he had come here this morning with that purpose in mind. About half of those from the Bible clubs came forward. Some got saved. Others returned from 'backslidersville'. One person came forward to volunteer his services there. Al felt as though he had done something today. The summer had come to a glorious end. He had the feeling the whole time that all that he had participated in was the right thing. The Association hounded him all summer to do it all their way. Was this it?

A team from the college came in to do the fall revival. They performed some really fast, really young music. The young preacher preached four days of powerful sermons. They also brought in their own soloists. Al MC'd the whole thing and he performed a lot of counseling. More people from the Bible clubs made decisions. Al asked himself who made these revivals come together. Was it him or the Association or was it both, together? How was it possible he could work this closely with those people?

The Harvest party was a thriving success. Some kids came in costume, though. Who told them to do that? It was more than likely the result of a compromise with the children on the part of the parents. Some of the costumes were demonic but most were half-way descent. But, absolutely no prizes for best costume or candy give-aways. He looked around for anything giving the indication of Halloween. What, was that a goblin over there? Do they not understand the concept of a Harvest party? It's October 31ˢᵗ but it's not Halloween. Tomorrow, they would celebrate the day known as "All Saints' Day".

The remainder of the year was filled with Christmas decorating, a big turkey dinner, dramas performed by both children and adults alike from churches around the Association and don't forget the caroling. He also distributed toys to all of the children who came looking. He let it all go for the holidays. He didn't do any more work than was required of him. As a matter of fact, he may even have put on a few pounds. It was difficult to determine. He didn't care, anyway. He was living the life he intended to. It would all put an end to his year.

And all of the next few years would end up like that. He taught in the winters, do his benevolent ministries in the spring, Bible clubs in the summers, and revivals and harvest parties in the fall. And then always came the Christmas celebrations. He ran things around there entirely on his own. He was in charge and everybody knows it. He even got good with the volunteers. He put Bob in charge of all of the decorating. (Not Alice's Bob) He got Alice to begin helping with the Bible clubs. And every year one of the churches, except one, gave them an extra week. And that one church always encouraged kids to dress up for the harvest parties.

After five years of doing the job without Carol, he was finally over the whole situation. But, he was still angry with the Association. His anger, though, had little to do with Carol leaving, not now. His resentment of them was in regard to something else. He thought he knew what that was. But he just didn't, or wouldn't acknowledge it. He accepted the fact she was gone. He was fine being alone. So, what made him so angry with them? Why was he so bitter? Where was this resentment coming from? He knew, all right.

HER

1

He came in and sat at his desk. On it in front of him was an envelope with his name on it. It was from the Association office. What were they after? His annual report had been submitted yesterday, with the same usual interruptions. But, what was this? If they had a problem with his report, someone would have called. Oh, wait, was it his walking papers? No, once again, somebody would probably have come over for that. What was it? He didn't even want to open it. But, he had to. He just had to know what was in this envelope. He flipped it over to see how he could open it. He opened it and pulled out the contents.

There were three different documents. The first was a letter from the Association. It was addressed to him. It was from the Human Resource Department. It seemed to speak of a possible new face at the mission. It told tale of a young woman named Stacey Hague. The letter requested a time for an interview. It asked for a time *when* he could interview her. Whatever happened to *if*? What is *when*? Has she already been chosen?

The next document was a cover letter. He was prepared to read a 'not so good' one. He hoped it would say something like,

"Dear Sir, I hope we can talk about a job…there, wherever you're at. I don't know, maybe a job or something, I don't know. Maybe we could do one of those…interviews…or something…I don't know."

He wanted to throw the whole thing out. But what sat before him, instead, was indeed a work of literary art. It was arranged in perfect order. It presented an introduction of the candidate. It spoke of an impressive education and church work history. It was good, indeed.

The final document was the resume. Oh, but of course the resume won't match the cover letter. The work history will probably be weak. It'll probably reflect a job here for a few months, a job there for a couple of months, and finally some baby-sitting gig she did in the eighth grade. And her education will probably reveal her to be a high school drop-out, GED pending. But, once again, he was wrong. It showed, instead, that she possessed a Bachelor of Divinity degree, and then a Master's degree. And there were churches listed in her work history.

Well, he'll show them. He'll place it back in the envelope and conveniently forget about it. After all, just when did they do the hiring for him? Did he miss that meeting? Yeah, he probably did. He purposely missed a few Association meetings. They never seemed to discuss issues at the mission. It was always First Church this and FC that. And it was always money, money, money. No, he wouldn't call them about her and they would probably just forget about it go on with things. Yes, that's right, just sit back and forget about it.

The ring of the phone would prove to change all of that.

"Al Bryant here."

"Al, this is Phil with Human Resources at the Association. I was just wondering if you received a letter we sent regarding a young woman, Stacey Hague.

It sounded like he had to do some research just to know her name.

"Anyway, I was wondering when you plan to interview her."

When? Not if?

"Phil, isn't interviewing more your job?"

"We've already spoken with her. We just need for you to fill her in with the details of what she would be doing."

"Well, I haven't decided I want her here."

"That's really not your decision, Al."

It's not?

"Fine, I'll let you know."

The ball was back in his court. He was in charge again. Yeah, he'll let them know all right. Now, when is he going to interview her? How about...Never! Oh, yeah, he had this. Let's see, what's her phone number? What's her name? Phil didn't even know her name. I know, as soon as Phil can call with her name at the tip of his tongue, where he just blurts it out, then, maybe, he'll think about... *considering* interviewing her, maybe. No, probably not. After all, they completely overlooked the obvious choice.

Yeah, why wasn't Carol offered this job? It was hers, after all. They laid her off (okay, it was five years ago, but still...). She should have just walked back through those doors, like she never left in the first place. But, who would he rather see walk through that door? Isn't there someone else? It just doesn't make any sense. Why give Carol's job to someone else? Did they even advertise a job opening? They certainly didn't consult him for advice on this.

If they had, he would have said,

"Carol. Bring Carol back!"

Ahh! It's lunch time and they haven't called back to confirm his scheduled appointment with...this...young...lady. She's probably a spy anyway. They probably dragged her out of some church, no doubt First Church, to keep an eye on him. That settles it. There's no way she's working here. What nerve to bring in someone to tell to all who would listen. She's probably wearing a wire. Every word he could say to her would be recorded, somewhere. If she wears glasses, they're probably fitted with a camera.

He made it! He made it to five o'clock! There had been no more mention of her for the rest of the day. It must be up to him, after all. She couldn't get the job if he didn't talk to her first. And he would not interview her if he could successfully avoid Phil. How about not coming in tomorrow at all? That way he could avoid any more of their checking his status regarding…what's her name. He will simply ignore her resume and, eventually, it will dissipate into thin air, as though it never existed at all. Oh, she will exist somewhere else. As will anyone else who tries to take Carol's job.

At home that evening, he sat down to some football on television. Football, a man's sport indeed, but mostly to watch and not to play necessarily. Although, it was rather enjoyable to pretend you were the quarterback or whoever was your hero. He often wondered how good a bowler any of these football stars were. Could any of them bowl at all? But he also wondered after their spiritual conditions. He'd heard of a few. How did they live their lives outside of the gridiron? And, they played on Sundays, so How did they go to church?

That night he had a dream. He dreamed that Carol came back to get her old job back. But, lo and behold, Phil was on sight to send her away. Then he spotted some very young woman working, in his office. He checked the name on the door and it wasn't his. *He* didn't even work there anymore. He argued with Phil but Carol interrupted, on Phil's side. What, was she kidding? What's that? Carol hadn't come here to get her job back. She was there to help remove *him* from *his* job. She was on their side. That girl…in his office…ha put…him…out…of…a..job!

He awoke on Tuesday very tired. No, he wasn't going in today. Can he do that? If he goes in, they'll call. If he doesn't, they'll still call but he won't have to know about it. What's the difference? His answer will still be the same no matter what. He has not set up the interview, and he won't. But, where to go, to hide? Hey, visitation isn't going to work but it's his job. Where will he go? Hey, why not look into the Bible study that's been going on at the jail? Yeah, he'll visit the prisoners as Isaiah said.

Out for breakfast first, donuts. He knew right where to go. It was down the street from the mission. Dangerous, right? He was risking being seen. But, if someone saw him, they would probably assume he was on his way to work. Wait a minute. This place was close enough to work, it was like he was there. Then, he leaves (work) to go to jail, to the jail, and it's just like he's at work. Only, he doesn't have to hear the phone ring. And that's too bad because...? Oh, they can't find him. And they don't want to. If he inquires of them her name, they won't even know it.

He pulled up to the gate outside the jail. A guard met him at his car. He produced proper credentials and was directed inside. He parked right where it said 'Clergy'. How nice to have your own parking space at a space such as this one. They expect you but only because it's only a part of the whole scene. It's not because they actually respect what you do or even want you there. After all, it's just another excuse for inmates to get out of their cells. Their day would be so much easier if they could just leave them laid up in their bunks all day.

He had to pass through several locked doors before finally arriving at the chapel. He also had to undergo a search, like he was attempting to smuggle in...something, who knows what! Although, a clergy did once smuggle in a make-shift key made out of a cross. He had sharpened the bottom end of it. What was he thinking? Al knew what he had been thinking. The inmate's partners (codefendants) on the outside had his family in their crosshairs. He was forced (extorted) to do it. No, that didn't really happen. That was on a made-for-tv movie once. But, it was always better to be safe than sorry.

They escorted him to the chapel. There he found the Bible study going on as he had expected. It was being conducted by a pastor of one of the churches in the Association. He and his music minister conducted a service for the inmates. They really seemed to appreciate it. He entered and was welcomed warmly. Wow, he could stay in this place. He felt appreciated here. He knew he provided an excursion for these guys. He provided for them an opportunity to get out of their cells for about an hour.

They requested prayer for family and friends on the outside. They didn't seem to care as much about their own situations. Maybe, deep down, they accepted that they were where they needed to be right now. Some did, however, request prayer over upcoming court dates. One guy was waiting for a verdict back on his case, another awaited sentencing, while still another was due to go to prison soon. The guys who were getting out soon rarely came to these services. It was a shame what it took to get the attention of some of these guys. They had to learn the hard way. And this indeed was a hard way to learn. Some inmates were killed recently in a brawl over food, and others just lost hope.

Just before the service was to end, the guards entered and proceeded to escort the inmates back to their cells. They requested of the ministers to please remain in the chapel due to some *issues*. They promised to allow them to leave when the *issues* were taken care of. It was a little scary, but invigorating. It also proved interesting. They could hear yelling and cussing, along with threatening. He wasn't worried, though, because he knew that none of them had any *issues* with him. But, still, being locked in this room while a riot was going on…

And, just as his head was about to explode with claustrophobia, the guards returned with the 'all clear'. As it turns out, an inmate had thrown his tray of food…that's all. An inmate got thrown on his face, hand-cuffed, hog-tied, and thrown into solitary confinement. Al just hoped they at least untied him after they placed him in the confinement cell. Oh, well, he guessed that's what he gets for throwing his tray. Al had considered doing the same thing a few times at the mission. Would they hog-tie him? Or, would they expect him to hog-tie himself since he was in charge? What sort of silly thinking is this?

And speaking of throwing trays and the cafeteria at the mission, he was hungry and it was lunch time. He had appreciated the opportunity he had been given to eat decent food and walk out of the jail. He wondered after that place where the guards spoke of having eaten at frequently. He considered stopping there. It was more than likely a greasy spoon, but he liked those, didn't he? There was a time he had not been able to go to places such as those. But, those days are long gone. It's now hamburgers and onion rings.

He drove to, no, not to but by the office, on his way... home. He did not return to work. Instead, loaded down with a ton of guilt, he headed for home. He honestly tried to put the mission behind him. What is avoidance going to accomplish? It's going to fill him full of guilt. Oh, I know, he can go home and rest up for a full day tomorrow. He'll be at that place to work during the day, eat dinner, and teach at night. No more guilt. Just drive fast all the way home. Avoid those pesky people who are trying to hire people behind his back. And not the correct people either. But, what if it were her? Her who?

He went home. He settled in. He began to think, to ponder... about his bicycle.

'Go for a ride?' he thought.

'Why, yes, I think I shall.'

Dogs barked at him. That was normal. It was cold, but not windy. He had his coat on. What a great time he had on his bicycle. But, soon he was tired. So, he stopped at a store. He bought some juice. Then he proceeded back home. But, first, the ice cream man. In the winter, he didn't have to compete with those pesky kids.

Once home, he took a nap. It felt good to sit in his chair with the sun shining through his window. A nap in the middle of the day with a clear conscience is exactly what he deserved. They didn't know whom they were fooling with.

'Ha! Ha! I'll bet they're looking for me.' he thought.

'They can't find me and they want to give Carol's job away.'

She doesn't even know the job is available again. They are keeping that from her. He should call her and tell her. Yes, he will do that. But, it's just a nap. He may be dreaming. He can't call her in a dream. Or, can he?

He awoke at approximately seven and removed a tv dinner from the freezer. He put it in the microwave and turned on the tv because it only makes sense to do so with a tv dinner. He watched some crazy show and ate his boneless rib meal and washed it down with a can of soda. He still wanted to call Carol about the job opening. Oh, what a shock when she arrives and the position has been filled, by her. That poor young lady will have to find a new job. Obviously, she doesn't belong here. She should be somewhere else.

Oops! He did it again, fell asleep in front of the tv. He awoke to one of those late night talk shows. He wished he would quit doing that. But, oh, the freedom in it. Of course, now he wouldn't be able to sleep tonight. For some reason, he looked out the window. It was snowing. Oh, yeah, it is winter. That's why, tomorrow, he would spend his daytime writing a lesson. And then he would eat his dinner with all of those who *might* attend the Bible study. The snow was peaceful. But his conscience wasn't. He found no peace with ignoring this girl's qualifications.

He dreamed that evening about what this young lady must look like. College grad, single, athletic, young, too young. She's not Carol. She never could be. In his dream, she was approaching the door. He decided to block the door. But then he remembered that she was a church rec major and suddenly she was pushing her way through the door and he couldn't hold her back, even if he did ride a bicycle. With the door between them, he couldn't actually see her. He could only imagine what she must look like. He imagined some large, green monster.

He woke up tired on Wednesday. He read his scripture and meditated as he listened to music. He thanked God that this young lady was so qualified and that she had not been sent to one of the churches instead of the mission. He confessed his rage against the powers that be. He prayed for this young lady to find her place. But that very prayer told him that this was her place. No, it wasn't. This was carol's place. Carol belonged here. Oh, no time to confess again. Someone else belonged here, but who? It wasn't this young lady. The Association seemed to think that she belonged here.

He arrived at the mission just to remember the letter and resume sitting on his desk. And, there would probably be a phone message waiting from yesterday, no, probably a hundred of them. He smiled, though, thinking of how it is that they must wait on him for this hiring of this poor young woman who's being placed in a place where she doesn't belong by who think they know more than God. That's bad. But, she is the victim here. She's the victim of a false calling (a calling made by man). Some people have told her she's called to something she's not.

The envelope still sat on his desk, along with other mail he hadn't opened. Well, yes, he had opened the envelope already. But, officially, as far as *they* were concerned, he hadn't. Officially, it sat on his desk, unobserved. No, he observed it. But, what did it really say? It said that a young woman with the correct qualifications was interested in the job opening (what opening?) at the mission brought about by a not so recent vacancy. Somehow, hers had bypassed the correct one. There was, after all, only one person for that job. Okay, so what about this other mail?

Enough pish posh, it was time to write the lesson for this evening's service. He just simply had no free time to look at resumes. He had a ministry to run here. People had high expectations for him here. How could he possibly conduct an interview, and then make an informed decision? Oh, yeah, they said he had no say in the matter. Well, we'll just see about that. If he doesn't conduct this interview, she can't come to work here. But, what are they going to do with her if he doesn't? She'll work for them, but not for him. She'll be in a state of flux, the poor girl. Oh, yeah, he almost forgot the lesson.

He went inside feeling powerful. He controlled a lot right now. He walked by Carol's empty office, thinking it would stay that way until they got smart and played his game. Bring Carol back. No one else belongs here. No, they're not listeneing. Bring Carol back, not this other girl. Continuing onward, volunteers milled around as he headed toward his own office. There it awaited his attention. But paying attention to it meant calling her. That meant maybe hiring her. And hiring her meant filling Carol's job. And that, in turn, meant saying good-bye.

He finished the lesson and looked at his clock. It was lunch time. Well, time to go eat. What? They expect him to look over the information on this girl instead of taking a lunch break? That's unbelievable. No, he's just not going to do it. That's slave labor. They can't do that. He's allowed a lunch break after all. How can he take a break in the middle of the day if he has to read her information? He can't, that's how! He won't! He got up and proceeded to the cafeteria. He ate alone. Was he trying to prove something?

After lunch, though, he was thrown into the dungeon. Wow, did I really just now radically change the whole theme of this book? The handsome young prince has been captured by the evil king and thrown into the dungeon. Woe is me! No, really, it's a dungeon of having plenty of time to read (reread?) her resume and cover letter. Oh, I know that he can ignore the letter from the Association and act completely puzzled by the reasoning her interest in this position. There are no openings here. No, kid, I'm sorry but the Association said they cannot afford two missionaries.

Then the afternoon rolled around. He was so proud of himself for thinking of that. Wait a minute! Was it their intention to cut his salary in half to hire this girl? He'd have to sell his car, move to a smaller place (Oh, wait, he lived in the parsonage.) Will they, then, move her in? She's the wicked witch. No, no, she's the victim here, remember? But, so is Carol? So is he. *They* are the evil ones. *They* say *they* can't afford two missionaries, but then *they* attempt to hire one.

Five o'clock arrived right on schedule. The day for looking at resumes and things was behind him again. Oh, the poor thing, she probably sat at home wondering why, once again, no one called about the job. She would sit by the phone ever so patiently, but no call. What has he done? The poor girl would have to wait until tomorrow. She would cry herself to sleep again tonight. But, what about Carol? She didn't even know. He should call her. But, somehow, that didn't seem like the solution, either. Why not? Shouldn't that action on his part solve everything? For an ultimate solution, however, it sure seemed empty.

He entered the dining room at dinner time. It was time to count heads and wonder who would be staying for the lesson. Let's see, there were probably a hundred people here tonight. Twenty-five would no doubt be leaving right after dinner. Did they not require spiritual feeding as well? But, he knew they'd be going home after dinner, eat and run. He kind of took it personal. Was it his teaching? Or, were they so convicted by the Holy Spirit that they just couldn't handle it? No, it's just the averages.

Then the seventy-five, or less, came into the chapel. He watched as they filed inside. He hoped both the young woman and Carol would be in church, somewhere tonight. He kind of felt a kinship with King David when he conducted the census. He watched them arrive, but he didn't count them (64). Oh, bu of course, all of those with children probably went home. Children's choir had not been conducted since the downsizing of Carol. He had considered asking the young man from Sunday morning if he wanted to take over the responsibilities of it. So, why had he not asked him? Because he was the lone missionary, that's why. No one could work alongside him.

He made announcements. He fielded prayer requests. He made jokes about the weather. But, he was keeping a secret. He imagined himself informing them of the young candidate for the job (Once again, what job?). You know, the job the Association didn't have the money to fill. Remember, Carol's job? Oh, and when he broke the news to them that Carol, their Carol (their friend) hadn't even been considered, they would riot in the streets. They might riot over that one. She hadn't even been considered. They completely left her out of the equation.

The lesson, oh, yes, the lesson.

He taught from the gospels. But every time he tried to make a point about bad people, he felt like one.

"The Pharisees…"

He was one.

"The Saducees…"

Yep, him again.

"The Roman Centurion…"

If only he could look like that.

He went home thinking about all of that. He couldn't escape all of those thoughts. He hadn't disclosed to the congregation that there may be a new missionary. He also did not communicate with the Association about his lack of effort on bringing in this new girl. He left her hanging. He kept it from Carol that she was being left out. He feared it would wound her deeply if she knew. He was keeping it all inside. That's why it hurt so much. He didn't talk about it, to anyone, at all. His confidant was gone from him.

That night he sat in his office at home, looking out the window. What has brought him to this place in his mind? He fought for control, not only of his ministry, but of himself as well. He was lying to people. He never did that before. Or, had he? He was keeping people out of the loop. Others, he was keeping out of a job. He lied to the people at the Association just by failing to set up a time to interview this young lady. She was well qualified. She could find a job just about anywhere. But, would that bring…Carol back? What exactly was going on in his cranium?

2

They made it through another winter. It was the easiest one they've had in a few years. He just knew that March would be rough as winter actually ends in this month. He had come to work on a Thursday. He hadn't heard anymore about that young missionary. He guessed she'd found something else to do. He hoped so, anyway. But, still, Carol didn't come back. So, it was true. They couldn't afford a second missionary. He laughed as he thought about the people at the Association running around like chickens with their heads cut off.

His laughter was interrupted by a knock at the door.

"Excuse me, sir. Are you Al Bryant? I'm Stacey Hague. I'm supposed to start work today."

He almost fell out of his chair.

"Today? Are you sure?"

"Yes, I was actually hired at the first of the year. But, I had to get a few things taken care of first. So, they said I had until today."

"I was Not under the impression that you had been selected. I mean, I had not interviewed you yet."

"Oh, uh, they did that at the...office.

He was perplexed, indeed. They had bypassed Carol completely and he had no control over it.

"Uh, Mr.Bryant, they informed me that you would call me with a day and time for me to come look around."

"Oh, I'm…"

"I'm sorry, sir. I hope you don't mind. I haven't actually been at that number in over a month. So, if you left a message, I didn't get it. But, (sigh) that's okay. Would you mind a whole lot showing me around today? Would that be all right?"

Yeah, sure."

If you can't beat them,…

He got up from his desk and proceeded to direct her attention down the hallway. He would definitely be calling Carol.

He couldn't believe he was doing this. He showed her around, starting at the clothes closet and then the food pantry. He said he would show her the cafeteria at lunch time. He also informed her that their meals were free there. She seemed so excited about every little bit of it.

'Don't get excited.' He thought 'You won't be here that long.'

He walked her around to the meeting rooms, the chapel, the hallway soon to be decorated for Easter, and everywhere else he thought she needed to see. She asked him about the gym.

Lunch time saved him on that one. He didn't want to delve into all of the gory details about the gym. But, maybe that story would send her screaming out of this place. After all,she did receive her degree in church rec. And if she couldn't do that Instead, he said that First Church had the only gym in the Association. That was the truth, but not the whole truth. Theirs was the only one in any kind of use. He gave her the times the café served meals. Her smile, and enthusiasm, had disappeared upon hearing the news about the gym. He couldn't believe he hadn't told her before. But, why had *they* hired her if *they* knew?

After lunch, he pointed out to her what would be her work space. She appeared a bit disappointed.

'Oh, no' he thought, 'are you disappointed?'

She inquired of him his expectations of her. That's when it occurred to him...

'She's his new report writer.'

She could do all of that report writing that he did not wish to do. This fell right into his lap. So, he broke the news to her.

He walked away, instructing her to come to him with any and all questions. He returned to her with all of the info she needed to get started, on all of that report writing. He felt so diabolical, so vindictive. But he also felt like he was doing her a favor by showing her just what the Association had done to her. They put her in a place she just didn't belong. There *was* no gym. And that's what she came here to do. They knew it the whole time and they didn't tell her. What had they told her? He would give her a week before she would just get up and walk out. He couldn't wait. He would, however, have to stop laughing before he called them.

Later, he performed his usual walk around inspection for the day. It had proved to be a peaceful afternoon. There had been a lack of pesky young missionaries asking questions. He walked by her office (which should have been Carol's). She seemed so bored, out of place.

'Poor thing" he thought.

She had been fooled into believing she would (could) serve a useful purpose here. They had failed to mention to her that there was no gym. That made no sense.

At the end of the work day, he told her it was quitting time. She thanked him with a look of despair. He assumed she was beginning her descent early. Her look seemed to say, quitting what?'

She was serving a purpose there. She took over report writing. The removal of that burden from his work load was a relief. He passed the buck, much as *they* had. He should call and thank *them* for his new...secretary. They would probably respond with...

"What!?"

It occurred to him, though, that it just might behoove him to actually show up for work tomorrow. If he failed to, they may give her his job. He'd have to be creative. Maybe he'd take her out on a visit (and leave her there?) He felt so vindictive. He could show her the old gym they closed down. He could show her the gym at First Church. But they were so picky about No, he didn't want to give her any purpose here except to do what it was he didn't care to do. That was mean.

He had a rough night. Some craziness was inside of him. What had he done to this poor girl? He had a difficult time living with all of this. Guilt tore away at his soul. He needed to call Carol and break this awful news to her. Without even consulting either her (or him), they hired this girl instead of even offering the job to Carol (or back to Carol). Oh, the tears. Carol would simply fall apart. She would slip into despair and live the remainder of her existence in mediocrity. He bet Phil was feeling pretty awful proud of himself right about now. He got his way. He got his way by lying to this poor girl.

It occurred to him that she didn't look anything like she did in his dream. She was a pleasant looking young woman but with an athletic, boyish quality. She definitely did not look like someone who might feel comfortable in an office at a desk doing menial paperwork. She looked like someone who probably went out for a run that morning (it was Friday, after all). He was sure she stayed healthy and ate right. How dare she tell him how to eat and exercise. No doubt about it, she had to go. But she would be glad she did.

He went to work. Oh, boy, she had probably called Phil last night after work to tell on him.

"He's not utilizing my gifts and talents,' she would say.

His reply, "I'll give him a stern talking to."

"Thank you, sir."

"Anytime, little lady."

And now, Black Bart (Al) will walk into the saloon (the mission).

She was hard at it. She seemed to be writing as he walked by. He really should be friendly.

"Good morning," he quipped.

She looked up from her work.

"Good morning, Mr. Bryant."

"Al, please."

"Al, hi."

"Hello."

He actually read a book as he sat in his office. There was no work to be done today. He could conduct visits, but it's so cold out there as spring hasn't set in yet. His book began to put him to sleep. He nodded off and caught himself over and over again. He could also take a nap today. Wow, wouldn't that be something if a rep from the Association caught him napping on the job. That could be the very excuse they've been waiting for. No, he'd have to get up and walk around, something, anything to wake him up. But this book is so good. It's one of those Christian fiction books by one of his favorite authors. If only this guy would put out more books.

He got up to walk around, but he walked all the way outside. He hadn't been out there in a while, except to get in his car and drive home. He walked all the way around the building. How many laps could he do around the building before stopping for lunch? He'd never seen the back of the building. Oh, wait, yes he had. He'd been back there before, for deliveries to the kitchen. But it had been such a long time. Has anything changed? He walked back toward the kitchen. He could smell the grill from out there.

He walked around until lunch time. Then he went back inside and went straight back to the cafeteria. Stacey was sitting in there with her soup and sandwich, working through lunch.

"You don't have to do that", he interrupted.

"Oh", she replied, "I just wanted to get it done."

"Oh, no hurry."

"Okay, thanks."

He walked away.

He tried reading after lunch. Once again, though, he kept nodding off. So, once every hour (sometimes half hour) he got up and walked around. I worked great until he decided late in the afternoon to utilize the pop machine. Great, caffeine, exactly what he needed. And the sugar should prove helpful in keeping him awake. Oh, Friday, what a day. But, from now on, this is what his Fridays will look like. He should take a vacation but it probably would not be allowed with a new employee to train.

At quitting time, he wished his protégé a good weekend and invited her to the service on Sunday. What could a Rec major possibly contribute to a worship service? What contribution can she possibly make here at all? They did have a gym but it got closed several years ago. So, why did they send her? What were they thinking? Were they thinking? They must have been thinking of something. They were probably thinking that they did not want Carol.

They said, in unison, "Anybody but Carol."

He was sure of it.

Forget going home. He headed straight for the bowling alley. Dinner would be a greasy burger, pepperoni pizza that tasted like cardboard, or maybr soggy nachos with plenty of jalapeno. He didn't have to get up on Saturday for anything. He had to put this girl behind him. Greasy food and soda, along with bowling should assist in that endeavor. He could have invited this Rec major but he didn't want her to get the wrong idea. What if she thought he was asking her out? He couldn't allow that happen.

She was a well kept secret. She had to be. After all, she didn't actually exist. That was Carol's job and she wasn't there to do it. So, nobody actually occupied that office. His denial was legendary. But, what if she stayed? What if they replaced him with her? That's another thing he couldn't allow to happen. Suddenly, though, he feared for his job. But, he couldn't let that be known for a couple of reasons. One, it was ridiculous to suspect she *could* replace him And, second, he couldn't allow the Association to know they had him on the ropes. He couldn't allow them to think they had any control of him, that he feared them.

She was there, in attendance on Sunday morning. Honestly, he wouldn't expect any less. He was actually happy to see her. This is something he can allow her to do. She could attend church here. She didn't interact well, though. She seemed out of place. Of course she was. This was Carol's place. She had Carol's job. These were Carol's people. Besides that, why didn't they feel the same way as he did? Or, did they? Was she a sheep among a pack of angry wolves? He felt sorry for her if she was.

It was several months later, now in summer. His young protégé didn't seem to smile very much. He didn't know why she stayed. He sure wouldn't have. He would have left a long time ago. He just kept her at that desk, writing reports. He wanted to feel sorry for her, but he also wanted her to quit. He still hadn't gotten over how she just showed up one day without his permission. They hired her behind his back. Carol was supposed to be doing her job, not her. But that look on Stacey's face, it made him sad.

He came to work on Monday. He was excited about the Bible clubs coming up. Once again, as usual, one of the churches gave them an extra week. This year they would have the seventh and tenth week of the summer. A different group of volunteers entirely showed up for this one. He went ahead and allowed Stacey to lead the games. He just couldn't stand seeing her skills go to waste. But he had to be careful that she knew he was in charge. There would be no usurping his authority by this one. Even though, he didn't really think she would.

His lunch on that day was at a large, buffet style restaurant. Ministers from all over the Association as well as a few others ate there on Sundays. He talked with and got along with a lot of them. Some of them, though, acted toward him as if he were doing something evil at the mission. Some had said in the past that having church there was like telling people they didn't have to attend anywhere else in the area (like in a real church). And there was also all of the social work he did out there. They felt like he didn't encourage people to work.

She took off the week of July fourth to go see family. He kind of missed her. He thought, as well, that if she were gone he wouldn't feel as guilty. He was wrong! He felf even more guilty. What if she did not return? What if something happened to her? Perish the thought of that. But, if she didn't return, what kind of person would be hired to replace her? There were, he ahd to admit, a lot worse candidates out there. She was (swallow hard) really pretty good for this job.

The holiday fell on Tuesday. So, he wouldn't be expected at work. He slept like he hadn't in a while. But he dreamed about her sad face, his guilty conscience, and all of her wasted talents and education. But carol never entered his dreams. He felt like he was caught in between a rock and a hard place. Carol, who belonged there was completely ignored and he was supposed to work with someone who didn't belong there. He had to both know that and simply put up with it. He had no power or control of anything at all. That's why he was bitter.

He just walked on that day. He got out of bed, threw on his clothes, and went outside with no particular place to go. There would be no ministry today. He just walked and walked and walked. But he couldn't manage to walk off his guilty conscience. He kept thinking about the girl and how she looks so sad just sitting there at that desk, filling out reports. If she would just get up and storm out of there, blaming the Association for doing her wrong. They put her in the wrong place But, Carol never seemed to blame them. What was the deal with these women? Did they not believe in passing blame to others?

He found donuts and coffee at a bakery. He ahd walked himself hungry. And he loved donuts. He also loved coffee. That was his guilty pleasure. Well, it was one of them. There were others and he may partake of one or two of them today. He had already made plans to attend a picnic and fireworks show. He was free to do as he pleased today. He was certain all the folks at the Association were probably at home today, unconcerned about what it was he was doing today. All was on pause today.

His walk in the park was soothing. Families were everywhere.

Kids played, probably not thinking yet about the fireworks. But they would all go see them somewhere. The parents would make sure of that. Al always worried, though, about children being kept up that late. It was only one night, but still. Some older people gathered around an area where a lot of pigeons came around to. They were group of senior citizens who like feeding the pigeons. Others complained, however, because feeding them contributed to them doing their business on windshields. And then there were the teens who rode skateboards and bikes in the park.

Lunch was at a hot dog stand. He had two, some chips, and a can of pop. He found a park bench to eat at. The stand had proved to be a popular source of food at this noon hour as several people seemed to have the same idea. He didn't mind, though. He enjoyed the company. That's why he had gone into ministry in the first place, his love for people. But, somewhere along the way, he had lost some of that. What exactly happened to offset his joy?

That afternoon, he happened to see Bob and Alice. They had the kids, who were all growing like weeds, out there for the festivities. He watched these kids grow up like they were his own. In a way, they were. God had entrusted all of them to his spiritual care, for teaching and preaching, worship. He enjoyed that responsibility. By the way, Alice's little tag-along had grown a little more independent as he began to follow the older ones along. He did, finally, grow up enough to understand what had happened to Bobby. He cried the day he figured it out, as did the child.

A little later, Al got another can of pop and some ice cream. He sat and looked at the lake as he reflected on all that was going on. He also said a prayer for everyone there that day. He prayed they would seek freedom from the power of sin and death. He prayed they would desire to be independent in their giving over to Christ. So many soldiers had given all so that everyone would have the right to appreciate it.

Around seven, barbeques began putting out burgers and dogs, along with chicken, steak and ribs. They also cooked potatoes and corn on the cob. Al got a great big plate of food and sat with some people that he knew. He enjoyed himself as he talked and laughed, thinking nothing of the mission and the newcomer. All he did was eat and visit. People laughed. Nobody asked questions. He was glad of that because he feared they would inquire of …her. Who was she? Where did she come from? What was she doing there? Why was Carol not there instead? No, wait, that was his question.

He must needs go to the boys' room before the fireworks commence. He hated using the lake bathrooms but choice did he possess, really? He could smell it a mile away. It was like nobody ever cleaned it, at all. Well, that was probably pretty accurate. And, with how busy the park had been that day, it surprised him not at all just how stinky it was. Oh, yuck, was all he could think of to describe it. Not to mention the writing on the wall was very…suggestive.

The fireworks were being set off across the lake from the park. He located just the right spot from which to take in the show. He peered around and spotted several people he knew. But he didn't see her. That was because she didn't belong there. No, not her, Carol. Carol was long gone, so stop thinking about her. But, it wasn't even her he was thinking about. Just, who was it? He sat and watched the night sky as rockets exploded from gunpowder. He saw all the beautiful colors and heard all the loud kabooms along with the oohs and aahs of others. And he sensed something like a phantom at his side.

All the necessary reports got filled out in June by her. He felt sad as he imagined her telling her family that all that she ever does is fill out reports, basically wasting her skills. But, would she also tell them all how the Association placed her into the wrong job? He hoped she would make them out as the bad guys instead of him. He could just imagine what their opinion of him would be after talking with her. Yes, he was a cad, but he was doing the right thing, right? It sure didn't feel like it. She was suffering. Carol was suffering. He was suffering. The people at the mission were suffering.

3

The fall revival was a success. Or, at least those at the Association thought so. There were, apparently, enough decisions made to justify all of their efforts. He guessed they thought their money was justifiably spent. The numbers told the story. Or, did they? No, they really didn't. There were personalities involved and a number of different types of decisions. It kind of seemed as though some of the rededications were more a promise not to sue.

Sometimes, someone gets saved in a church. But the church fails in its obligation to follow-up and disciple them. So, they have no reason to live-for Christ. They instead live just for self and they fall away. They don't lose their salvation but they quit growing in Christ likeness. And, when you're not growing, you're dying. So, instead of suing the church for neglect, they rededicate instead.

But, what the Association sees is someone who is guilty of sedition, but has returned for a second chance and they see second chances as though people were admitting the church never did anything wrong. So, it doesn't matter that the church failed in its follow-up obligation. Jesus said to make disciples, be witnesses, teach, and baptize. He never said to bring anyone to salvation. You can lead a horse to water but you can't make him drink.

He didn't even say to lead others to Him. That's a personal decision made by individuals. Repent and be saved, that is said in the Word. Belief and confession are also emphasized. But those are personal decisions. You can't measure that in numbers. You can count how many baptisms. But you can't peer inside the mind and heart. You don't know the sincerity of another.

None of us can know for certain if someone actually got saved or not. The powers that be require numbers to justify their money allotted to your ministry. And they base all of that on the number of baptisms.

And, speaking of the powers that be, then came the harvest party held every year at the mission. Some (one more than others) of the churches hold Halloween parties. But Al never believed the church should worship Satan. And they all resent the stand that he tends to take on that issue.

He believes, instead, in the celebration of how much God has blessed them throughout the year. But, mostly, he likes to celebrate all of the saved souls in the year. A bunch of them got saved at the revival in September. It's a time of celebration. He brings in a band from the college. They have a hayride (not a haunted one). And everybody has fun.

They serve a big dinner at Thanksgiving. People from all over his parish come in for turkey, potatoes, gravy, rolls, everything including cranberry sauce and pumpkin pie. Afterward, the kids played in the playground and the volunteers, who had served the meal, cleaned up afterward. The fellowship was a blessing.

A group from the college came in and worked with all of the kids on a Christmas program. And, as usual, the mission handed out toys to the kids. They also did a secret santa for the adults, where volunteers would buy a gift for a woman or a man and it would be given out on different days. Everybody just seemed to get into the holiday spirit.

During this time, Al was sitting in his office when a delivery man came to his door with a package. There was nothing new or different about this, especially at this time of the year. Al had a grown daughter whom he did not see or hear from anymore for some reason. Well, actually, he knew why.

But the package wasn't from her. It was from Carol. He became a bit angry because he was under the impression that they had agreed not to exchange gifts. She usually sent him a card but this year it was a package. He wasn't sure whether to open it or send it back. No, sending it back would probably hurt her feelings.

So, he began to open it when he saw the words:

'FRAGILE:HANDLE WITH CARE.'

Wow, what could it be? He was really angry now. But he couldn't help but think about how lucky he was to have such a good friend.

He opened it ever so slowly. He was afraid to use a knife on it. So, he utilized the scissors from his desk to cut the tape. He could see through the opening at the top of the box that it was gift wrapped. Great, this wasn't Christmas day. He'd have to wait until then. Would she even care? After all, she's not here. Neither is his mother. His father would allow it.

Well, it wasn't Christmas yet but it was Christmas time. There were twelve days of Christmas, after all. It was close enough. So, he finished opening the box. The gift wrapping was typical Carol wonderful. It was baby blue with holly and snow scenes all over it. He ever so carefully removed it from the outer box. Then he promptly discarded the box. After all, the box itself wasn't fragile. He felt like a member of the bomb squad. He handled it with kid gloves. The biggest reason for that was that it was from Carol. He placed the present square on his desk. He thought,

'What a thoughtful gift!'

He carefully began to unwrap it. It had a nice bow and some ribbon on it. He didn't want to destroy anything. he had been known before for his roughness, his gruffness. But he unwrapped this gift with kind consideration. This seemed to require more attention to detail than anything had in a while.

He finally managed to remove the wrapping, and what did he

discover? It was another box. Oh, the humanity, he had another box to open. This one was more personal than the one before. That one had been a mere delivery box. This one had that personal look to it. This one had come from her, personally. It was her box.

Once again, he employed the handy desk scissors. He knew he'd have a good use for them some day. He'd been using them to open mail. But then someone gave him a letter opener. It looks more like a weapon from a mystery show. He didn't want, however, to jab that thing through the tape in fear of what other damage it may do.

He finally got it open and he saw wood. It was finished wood. He reached ever so carefully into the box and removed the present. He pulled it up to where he could see a round face encased in a brown stained frame. It was a clock, a shelf clock to be more precise. He couldn't wait to put it on his shelf. He was careful not to accidentally bump the corner of the desk as he went around it. He did not want to drop it on the floor and …scratch it.

Sweat covered his forehead as he nervously carried the clock to his book case. His floor was carpeted, so he feared snagging his foot in the shag. He made it to the shelf. The available space was above his head. So, set it down and obtain a small foot stool? Where would he set it down at? Oh, what a predicament he found himself in. He could reach the shelf with the clock. But, what if it fell? No, no foot stool, a careful reach instead.

It looked so good right there. It was like it belonged there. It gave his office such an elegant look. He wasn't sure if he like that or not. He never saw himself as the elegant type. If he were, he'd be working at one of the other churches. That's where the elegant preachers were. But it did look good.

He looked at it every day through the holidays. He missed it during his time off. He never looked at another clock again. It were as though it was his only time reference. It had a face, like on that cartoon movie he had seen once. It almost spoke to him. But, what was it saying?

On the second of January, it was saying his break from work

was over. He had to go look at it saying it was nine o' clock a.m. Stacey saw it too. She commented on how beautiful it was. He told her where he got it. And that's when it occurred to him to call the gift giver, Carol, and thank her.

"Hello", came the voice at the other end.

"Carol, this is Al."

"Al, so nice to hear from you!"

"And also from you!"

"How are you?"

"I'm doing good. How are you?"

"Real well!"

"How was your Christmas?"

"Blessed, I am so blessed. How was yours?"

"It was good. I got the clock. Thank you!"

"You are very welcome. Where'd you put it?"

"I put it in my office."

"Where at?"

"On the book shelf..."

"Oh, good. That way you'll see it every day."

"So, how are things where you are?"

"Real nice! How about you? How are things at the mission?"

This is where he would have to be honest with her and tell her that her job had been given away. How could he break the news to her that she had been totally overlooked?

Well, here goes. Get ready for the tears. Had he made a mistake in calling her? He was about to cry himself. She will probably go on and on about how they hadn't even called her.

"Carol, I'm afraid I have bad news."

That's when he remembered the last time he called her with bad news, a young boy she knew had drowned.

"Oh, no, Al. what happened?"

"Uh, nothing... bad. It's just that, well, they filled your position."

In his mind, they shared some sorrow and a little resentment, if only...

But, instead, she said,

"Oh, good. That's good to hear."

She sounded…relieved.

'Good, you said…good? How's that good? That's horrible! What do you mean, good?'

But, really, he said,

"Good?"

"Yes, I was concerned they might not find someone."

(He heard planes and air raid sirens, people shouting from the street)

"But, you weren't even considered…wait, what?"

(Something like reality set in, all of a sudden like.)

"Oh, they offered."

(A German bomber flew over London. A torpedo dropped from its underbelly, landing in the middle of the city.)

BOOM!

"They offered?" He swallowed hard.

"Yes, I turned them down."

(Japanese Zeroes fly in, dropping torpedoes on American ships. And at the same moment (in his mind), planes fly into some buildings, killing innocent people!)

BOOM! BOOM! BOOM!

"What? Why?"

"Al, after I left there, I took a sabbatical from ministry. I attended church. I was in a Sunday school class that I loved. It was real nice, but after about a year, I wanted to go back into it again. I prayed about it and thought about it and then one day the Sunday school Director asked me to help teach in Sunday school.

"You know I love teaching. And I live children. So, I went for it. And it was every bit the blessing I thought it would be. Well, I did that for a while until they asked me to work in the nursery. Those babies were the best. I just loved seeing them on Sundays. Those babies were my job, and my joy.

"Then, last year, they came at me with the position of Education Director. I could hardly fathom it but it seemed like the right fit. I just knew this was what God had called me to. Right after that, I received the offer to go back there. I carefully considered which job I would miss the most. I do miss you and the mission. But I would miss this more. Sorry, Al."

"Sorry, for what?"

"For not telling you then. I just wasn't sure how you would take it."

Imagine that. He didn't want to tell her she'd been passed up and she didn't want to tell him she'd passed it up.

"So, Al, tell me all about my replacement."

"She's about twenty-seven now. She arrived with a seminary degree."

"Oh, in what?"

"Church Rec, actually."

"Al, that's exactly what you need there."

He felt like he had been called into the principal's office. This part of the conversation had been leading to what he didn't want her to know... what he had done with this young lady's particular gifts and talents, her calling.

"So, Al, how's she working out?"

"She's doing real well."

"Is she getting things going with the kids' soccer and adult league stuff? Oh, Al, this is so exciting!"

"Well, no, she hasn't exactly been doing any of that."

"Well, what exactly has she been doing?"

"You know those periodic reports?"

"Oh, the ones you...

He could feel the mood change, even hear it.

"Oh, Al, you didn't..."

"I...don't know what to say."

"Why would you relegate her to such a task?"

"I thought they had passed you up for the job. I thought you hadn't even been offered."

"You thought! You thought! You thought! Is that all that matters to you?"

"Now I see where I was wrong."

"Well, what are you going to do now?"

He did it. He did what he was going to do. He walked into Stacey's office. She looked bored as she sat writing about the previous year. This was definitely not her calling. She was meant for more activity. She wasn't cut out to push pencils at a desk. She had majored in Church Rec. She was a recreational person.

He knocked before entering. She looked up at him. She seemed surprised to see him.

"Hi, Al. Come on in."

"Stacey, I need to talk to you."

She seemed concerned.

"Is something wrong?"

He sat in a chair beside her desk.

"Stacey, I'm sorry."

"For what?"

"For keeping you in here. For failing to utilize your gifts, talents, and education."

"Oh, I just thought this had been a time of teaching, training, orientation."

"No, I shouldn't have relegated you to this.

He waved his hand over the paperwork on her desk.

"You had lunch yet?"

"No, not yet."

They proceeded to the cafeteria. He felt awkward walking with her. At one time, he had wished she would walk out, walk out of the mission, walk out of the Association. He wanted to see their faces as they realized their error in judgment. But, now, he realized they had not made a mistake at all.

Upon retrieval of their lunches, they sat down.

"Stacey, I have a confession to make."

She seemed a little uncomfortable. Was he about to confess an attraction, a crush?

"Oh?"

"I relegated you to report writing because I thought the Association had forgotten Carol. But then I found out she had actually been offered first. I was angry. I wasn't mad at you. I was mad at the Association. But I took it out on you. And for that, I apologize."

"It's okay, Al. I forgive you."

He could tell that she meant it.

They talked through lunch. He got an idea. He invited her out to go see something the next day. He became immediately self-conscious, of his invitation. But she didn't seem to take it in any wrong way. She was, however, curious about it. But he couldn't help but feel like he preferred to show her. He knew she would like it. It was right up her alley.

The next day, they met at work. He took her out for coffee and donuts. But she ordered juice and a brand muffin. That was okay. He respected her personal preferences. He needed to begin to practice that daily now. She was his new ministry partner. Before they had left the office, though, he had grabbed a certain set of keys from his office. He hadn't thought that he would ever need them again.

They drove for a while until reaching a building just off the road. She would see what it was. It was a large building... a gymnasium. Who knew this even existed? Well, apparently, Al knew of its existence. But she was just now finding out about it. If only she had known before, what she could have done. But she had that opportunity now.

They walked together to the side door of the building. She was mesmerized by it. This was a gymnasium. She had played many a basketball game in one in high school and volleyball in college. She would later tell him about her desires to play football, but it was a male dominated sport. She was home now.

She began,

"Are those chains on the doors?"

"Yes, it was condemned about eight years ago."

"Why?"

"It seems one of the basketball goals got suspended in midair. They were afraid it would come loose and come crashing down some day."

"Sorry to hear that."

"Yeah, want to go inside?"

She looked at him incredulously.

"Are you sure?"

"It's okay to go inside. We just can't let people go in yet."

"Okay"

He used his keys to unlock the chain and then the door. She walked in behind him.

"It's probably kind of dusty in here."

"Okay, I won't breathe."

She was in awe as she looked around. He pointed to their left.

"Over there are the girls' locker room to the left and the boys' to the right. In the middle is the concession stand.

He pointed to the right.

"To the right over there is a little fitness area with exercise equipment. The office is in the middle."

He took her over to the office. She peered inside and saw a small desk and swivel chair, not much room.

"Perfect"

"Well, it's kind of an...but I guess a rec person wouldn't have a lot of use for an office.

She shook her head in agreement.

"But now (pointing left) for the pias de laresistance...

He opened a door and her eyes bugged out of her head.

"...basketballs, soccer balls, volleyballs..."

"and a net."

"Yes, and a net. But, also to your right is an electric air pump. The needles are probably in the desk somewhere."

As she looked it over, he said,

"Stacey, these are yours."

He handed her the keys.

"For me?"

"Welcome to your new office."

Oh, no, she started crying of all things. Then she hugged him.

"Al, this is wonderful. Thank you!"

"Well, you're welcome. But remember, you've got to get that goal fixed. I know someone who can help and I'll give you his number."

"Who is he?"

"His name is Rick. He grew up here and went off to college, obtained his Masters in Engineering. Now, he's a Civil Engineer in town."

"Great, thanks, I'll call him."

"Good, uh, Stacey, do you bowl?"

"I bowled in a league when I was in Seminary."

"I,m almost sorry I asked."

"Why?"

"Well, I meet with some...guys, older guys, well, my age...

She was careful not to respond.

"We meet on Friday nights in the city bowling alley. But you might show us up."

"I promise to go easy on you."

I appreciate that. But, the reason I ask is because one of them is Rick's father. He's a doctor. His name is Henry. Another is George. He's a lawyer. You can imagine the conversation gets involved. There's another. He's an army vet."

"Hey, my dad is a veteran of the Navy."

"You two should have a lot to talk about then. But I warn you, crude, except for Larry, the army guy. He's pretty nice, but real."

"I'm not concerned about all of that. With a Navy Captain father and two football player brothers, not to mention two old gruff grandpas and seven uncles…"

"Oh, belle of the ball."

She took a curtsy.

He was now relaxed the remainder of the week. He worked hard on Wednesday and Thursday. He didn't see Stacey but just for a few minutes. He was glad. He felt like she was in her element now. He was excited for her. She did, however, reveal to him a resignation letter she had saved on her computer. He had one, too.

Come Friday, he drove her out to the bowling alley. He told her she was welcome to come out every Friday if she wanted. She said she'd love to if the guys didn't mind. He said he didn't think they'd have a problem with that at all. As a matter of fact, they'd probably prefer she come without him.

They arrived and he promptly pointed out the concession area, warning her of the greasiness of the food. She didn't mind it once in a while. But, first, she wanted to meet the guys. He shook his head as he immediately regretted this. He saw them down a ways and pointed them out to her. She spotted three guys, all about Al's age and made a beeline for them.

Larry was the first to notice. He turned in his seat at the scoring table.

"Hello," she started.

Al came in close behind her.

"Gentlemen, this is Stacey. She works with me at the mission."

"Since when?" Henry asked.

"She's been there about a year."

Oh, no, here it comes.

"Best kept secrets...," George contributed.

She saved Al's neck, "Nice to meet all of you."

As they played, George remarked that Al had brought in a ringer. She played well and was admired by all. Even some others at the alley that night were admiring her skills. Some young men seemed to be admiring her. Al felt a little like a protective father on this one. It was a good feeling. He hadn't felt like that in a while.

Al mentioned at one point about her need to speak with Rick. But he didn't disclose as to why. Henry remarked about how she was barking up the wrong tree talking to him about Rick. His aunt had more influence on than he did, or ever hoped to, in those days. Al said he didn't think Rick would mind helping her out, although, he still failed to disclose any details.

When bowling was over, she said good-bye to her new found friends. That once sad, young woman now appeared happier than she had been in a long while. She seemed to bounce off the walls as they left. She was also very talkative as he drove her home. He was tired but she seemed to have her second wind.

Then, she asked,

"How do you know these gentlemen?"

He thought 'gentlemen?'

"We're all just old friends."

"Is Henry your doctor?"

"Yes, he is."

"We're all just old friends."

"Is Henry your doctor?"

"Yes, he is."

"For how long now?"

"Ever since I've lived here."

"Were you ever married?"

Where's this going?

"Yes, once, years ago."

"Do you care if I ask what happened?"

Could he drive while discussing this? No.

"No, I don't mind at all. But, we'll have to go for coffee. It's kind of a sad story."

"Oh, okay."

Of course, she would have juice.

They stopped at a truck stop and sat down for coffee and juice. He felt very self-conscious. He wondered if she felt the same. But what if everyone thought that she were his daughter? Yeah, that would work.

"Henry was my wife's and my doctor. My wife, Jenny, and I came to the mission 21 years ago. I had pastored a church for five years. I had been fired over some crazy politics. But this job came open and I came right over. We both wanted it and we worked alone for a while until Carol came in with us. She had been a member of First Church and she had a degree in church music. So, for five years it was the three of us.

"One day, she started feeling bad, my wife. She got to looking in the mirror one night and she called me into the bathroom.

Her eyes began to perk up.

"She thought she… felt…

He struggled. She stared at him.

"…a lump."

"Breast cancer?"

"Yeah, it was. I didn't want to think it."

"Yeah."

He started to suspect she might know something about this.

"Anyway, while I was in denial, she made an appointment with Henry. I could hardly move a muscle. I felt restrained by this whole thing.

He thought he saw her crying.

"I don't know why but I didn't want to take off work to take her to the doctor. But I didn't want her to go alone, either. I just didn't want to know. But she insisted. And I heard in her voice that she… needed me…there.

He started to cry himself and she was already there.

"Henry gave me a bit of a hard way to go about not having scheduled my usual checkup. I just said that she was his victim for the day. He was laughing then."

"Oh?"

"He took blood after he looked her over. Then he told us it would be a couple of days until he knew something.

He took a breath.

"I prayed for the best, knowing that what was…was. Then he called us. He asked us to come in and see him. I was becoming angry. It was supposed to all go away. But it wasn't going anywhere, any of it."

"What did he say?"

"Cancer cells."

"I'm sorry."

She touched his hand from across the table. The coffee was getting cold, as were the eggs.

"So was he. He wasn't his usual jovial self. He came into his office and revealed to us exactly what he had found."

"And then what?"

"He insisted that we obtain a second opinion. He referred us to an Oncologist in the city. I felt like I had no control of anything anymore. I didn't feel like I had any choices anymore. We had to see the specialist. I didn't want to hear what he had to say. It just wasn't going away.

"But she trusted Henry and all these other doctors. She wanted to make the appointment. It was almost like she wanted to hear that she was going to die. It was like…she wanted to die, to leave me alone…without her.

He thought about how much that reminded of his feelings about what happened to Carol.

"We made the appointment and time just dragged along. Work wasn't helping me to forget. I couldn't concentrate. I kept thinking about everything I had taken for granted. I just thought that she would live forever.

She did.

"I thought we'd be together forever.

"The day of the appointment finally arrived. She stayed close to me the whole time. I was scared to hold her. It felt as though I was giving her a hug good-bye if I did hold her. And I wasn't ready to say good-bye. But I felt like she *was* ready, somehow.

He seemed to have an 'I' problem.

"He took some samples. He referred to them as cultures. He said he'd get back to us in a few days with the results. I happened to talk to Henry during that time. He informed me that if he *calls*, it's probably good news. But if he requests our presence, it's probably not good. He had some experience with this.

She nodded her understanding.

"Once again, I was at work when the doctor called. He called Jenny. She called me. When she said he had called, I thought that meant that it was all good, it had all gone away. But she said he wanted to see us. I told Carol and she said to go, that she would hold down the fort. I thought 'Am I the only one who doesn't know?'

"On the day of, we made a day of it. We had lunch, talked, and laughed. I know what you're thinking. How could I be so jovial? It was her fault. She made me laugh. She was so much at peace. It drove me crazy. How could she…feel so good? We both knew what that doctor was going to say. But, how long would she have left? How long would we have left?

"When I was holding her hand, I couldn't help but notice her palms were sweating. She was actually nervous."

"Of course. She was human, after all. It's just a good thing you were there for her."

"Where else would I be?"

"No, you don't understand. I'm saying it's a good thing *you* were there."

He thought about that for a minute. He wasn't really there. He had existed during that time in a fantasy world where bad things go away if you spend enough time in denial of them.

"He gave us the very news we didn't want to hear.

"She lived just about a year after that. I took a lot of time off of work to be with her. She was so weak. I felt so helpless, powerless. I just wanted to fix it. She just wanted to be with me. It was all too real. I didn't want to say good-bye. But, I felt as though I were saying it every day.

"She had been in so much pain up until the end. But she was in so much peace after it was all over. To tell you the truth, she had seemed to be about that peaceful almost the whole time. But I'm still not at peace with any of it. I have to admit some resentment on my part about her peaceful spirit. I thought I needed for her to be at least a little resentful, just a tad might have been helpful but I couldn't count on that from her."

"How much time were you afforded afterward to grieve?"

"None, the Association said I had already taken enough time off. They barely allowed me enough time to bury her."

She looked reflectively away.

Then, "I had to get back to school."

"What?"

"My... my mom...died of...cancer...when I was in college."

"I'm sorry."

"But I took a summer, spent it in a grief group."

"I can't take time off."

"You will, at the right time."

He just let that go.

STACEY

1

I'm changing gears in the story here. I will concentrate on Stacey for just a while. Al will continue at the mission. But his partner will get her ministry in the gym going. I want the reader to see what was almost missed due to his resentful attitude. He gives her the phone number for the Civil Engineer in town and she will take it from there.

"Hello! This is Stacey. I work at the mission. Am I speaking to Rick?"

"Yes, this is Rick. How can I help you?"

"I have a mechanical issue I was hoping you could help me with."

"I'd be glad to try. Where do I meet you?"

"I'm at the gym on the old road."

"I thought they condemned that place."

"Some person, people, are looking to reopen it."

When she dropped Al's name to Rick, he seemed less reluctant, more pliable. He mentioned how long he'd known Al. She mentioned that she had met his father at the bowling alley. He chuckled at the thought of that. Before it was over, they had talked for an hour, or longer, she didn't know. But she didn't want to hang up.

She caught herself the next day thinking a man she'd only spoken to once. That kept happening all day. She worked around the gym. She organized her office. She found the needles for the air machine. She turned it on. It worked. So, she inflated all of the balls, including a real pig skin.

She carried her football out to the gym floor. She stretched with it at her side. She ran a hundred laps with it. She carried it through wind sprints. But she refused to shower with it. She got cleaned up and grabbed it up again. The shower water streamed from rusty faucets. But, for some reason, it was running.

She carried her new found companion into the concession area. She inspected it and found an old soda fountain along with some electrical outlets. She didn't trust them, although, the lights seemed to work all right. She would have to get Rick to inspect them. Oh, no, she was thinking about him again. She made a list.

She was actually nervous about meeting him. Him who? He's just another guy. Oh, I know, it's because of the nature of the meeting. She's about to see a dream come true. And he was going to help. So, what? That's all. He's not even a friend, not yet. He's merely someone will help her fix the basketball goal.

She made a peanut butter and jelly sandwich for lunch. She drank a bottle of water with it. She kept an ice chest there until she knew for sure the electricity would be okay. There was a pull-up bar in the gym and free weights in the work-out area. For some reason, though, she became self-conscience about sweat, smelling bad. Well, that was a first.

In the afternoon, she kept looking at the clock. She'd look, shake it off, and look again. He'll get here when he gets here. She hoped that, at least, he wouldn't be handsome. But, no, his dad was handsome. She could fall for his dad. She wondered what his mother looked like. What if she looked like her? It would be love at first sight.

Then, she heard a car pull up. Maybe it was just turning around. Maybe it was a member of the Association, there to kick her out. What if they chained the door? She'd be trapped forever. Rick would arrive, see the chains, become angry, and leave. What was this craziness? Should she look outside, no way!

He walked in. He looked around. He spotted her. He waved. He smiled. She waved. She smiled.

'This is business' she said to herself.

He is handsome. And he seems so nice. He's like his dad. He's getting closer to her. If Al hadn't recommended him so highly, she might not have invited him today. She might even fear him.

"Stacey, I'm Rick."

He extended his hand. She greeted him with the right hand of fellowship.

"Thanks for coming over."

"You're more than welcome. So, what's your concern?"

She pointed toward the wall. He went over to the crank. He looked inside it and nodded. He felt around inside of it.

He said, It's got a jam in the mechanism.

He motioned her over and pointed out the problem. She thought he smelled good.

"It's a gear. It's aluminum, so it bends easy. Somebody must have been messing with it."

"Yeah," was all that she had to say.

"I can fix it. It won't take much. It's a little rusty, but that's also easy to fix. Anything else I can do here?"

She handed him her well-thought out list. He looked it over and nodded positively. He said he would check out the water pipes and electricity. He sounded so confident, so reassuring. Her dad often sounded like that. Al had begun recently to sound that was as well.

For so long, she felt so alone, deserted. Now she knew why it had seemed like that. Al had explained it well. She could be mad at him. But after hearing about his wife, she totally understood. She related. She had been angry, and scared, during her mom's battle with cancer. But, she had experienced a sense of relief at her passing. That, she felt guilty over.

The two of them spent a few days together in the gym fixing

everything. He even had the authority to approve his own work. He had fixed the goal, the water pipes, and the electricity. She followed around behind him planning uses for things, things like a nacho chip distributor and a pot of cheese.

Then he asked her out.

"Huh?" she responded.

"Friday, bowling with the old guys."

"Yeah, sure, love to."

Did she say…love?

"Great, see you."

He picked her up Friday. She felt suddenly nervous because she felt as though she had leaped head first into something she wasn't ready for. But they talked the whole way there. She found out he had been the quarterback on the high school team. But he didn't get scouted. He was more interested in engineering anyway. He found it amusing to hear about her desire to play football because her brothers did.

"What did they play?"

"My oldest brother was a linebacker. The younger, still older than me, was a tight end. They were two years apart, though, so they didn't play together."

"So, what did you do?"

"I played basketball in high school and volleyball in college. I was in bowling league in seminary."

"Seminary, you have a seminary degree? In what?"

"Church Rec. I had a job while I was in seminary at an Associational skating rink."

"So, you like sports?"

"Love 'em!"

"What did your dad do?"

"Navy Captain, now he's retired."

"Your mom?"

"She was a homemaker until she passed, I was in college."

"I'm sorry to hear that."

"Thanks, it's been difficult, but mostly for my dad."

"Do you mind if I as what happened?"

"She got cancer."

"My aunt died of cancer."

"I guess that happens."

I am reinserting Al into the story at this point for a purpose. Why am I writing this in here? Because I feel like it. Also, I know that you're looking forward to seeing Al the story again. But, get ready. Things are about to get intesting.

They walked into the bowling alley together. Al was at the concession waiting on his (grease) burger and fries. The other older gentlemen were at the lane. Of course, Larry was at the scoring table. Father, Henry, sat at his usual spot, talking to his lawyer friend, George. He turned to see them coming in together.

"Richard?"

He stood in order to greet his son.

"Hi, dad, how's it?"

"It's just fine."

They shook hands.

"Hello, Henry," came Stacey.

He hugged her and said it was so nice to see them both. But he hadn't expected her to arrive alongside his son. He had no idea. He kept looking at his son. He hadn't pictured them together when he had met her. It definitely didn't bother him at all, though. He kind of smiled at it, actually. How cute!

Al came over and they set up the game. Everybody had their ball and shoes. There were six, three to a game. This was the biggest group they had in a while. They had a good time together. Al liked his new group of friends. George and Henry did their usual bit. Stacey enjoyed herself greatly. They were all like one big, happy family.

After the game, everybody stayed around visiting for a while. Al approached Stacey.

"Hey, you been all right?"

"Yes, I've been so excited, so motivated."

"Good, how's the gym?"

"Well, we managed to make a lot of needed repairs. I think it's ready."

"Now, we just have to get it approved."

"By who, exactly?"

"A few choice members of the Association."

"How do we go about that?"

"We plan a meeting."

Rick approached.

"Hey, Al, good to see you. I enjoyed tonight."

"That's great, Rick. Both of you come back next week. But, next time, the two of you can't be on the same team."

"Agreed."

He stuck out his hand and shook that of Al's.

Al explained to the both of them about the process of convincing the Association to allow them to open up the gym. In order to do that, they had to put together a proposal for the gym. Then they would have to get a few of them on their side beforehand. And, finally, they would deliver the proposal, which would include a speech beforehand.

Al offered to bring the speech. But he said that they would want to hear from her. But he also offered that there would have to be a meeting before the meeting with a few select members of the Association.

He said, "Call it a rally."

But, before that, the three of them would need to meet after the proposal is written up.

First, draw up the proposal. Then, come together for discussion and necessary editing. Then, they would meet with a few people Al thought would support their plan. Then, from that meeting, they could set up the meeting with the Association. That would be the big day.

So, the three planned a meet on Monday for brainstorming.

They would take notes and Al would draw it up. Rick seemed more than happy to help out in any way he could. They needed his expertise for details regarding electrical and mechanical issues. She would contribute plans for recreational activities. Al would write it up as he did that kind of thing well.

But, Saturday, as she ran and did her workout, she thought about…him. She got so confused she stopped running, realized she was running the wrong direction. She didn't even know what direction to run in. She had to finish her run, though. Should she call her dad? Why? Because that's what she always did before.

On Sunday, she attended services at the mission. The new music guy led the worship and Al preached out of the gospels. She felt a connection to Al. It was kind of a fatherly connection. He had informed her that he had one child, a daughter. They hadn't spoken much since his wife's passing. She couldn't imagine not having communicated with *her* father since her mom died.

She went home that afternoon for her usual chef salad lunch, with tofu as opposed to chicken. It had been such a good day to go to the gym, for a run. It was too chilly outside. And, what was that about an upcoming Valentine's Banquet? Oh, no, she would find it necessary to hide from…Rick until it was over.

She had plenty of time to think that evening. She pictured such sports as adult and child basketball, adult softball, water ballooning (fun), bowling, soccer, and volleyball. She got goose bumps just thinking about it all. But, she also considered the possibility of failure to convince the powers that be. But, how did Al put it?

'We do our best and pray for the rest.'

She thought about Rick coming in Monday for their brainstorming session. That little bitty office just won't hold the both of them. She considered her office to be out on the gym floor… anyway…so, move the desk…out…there, for now. She knew she could do so much more out there.

"Right on time," she said to Rick as he walked in.

"Right on time for what?"

"To help me move…

She pointed toward the office.

"…my desk"

He almost asked why but the tiny size of her office told the story. So, he helped her move it to the gym floor. He insisted she take the only chair available. Then they began to brainstorm ideas. She served as secretary as she wrote ideas down on a legal pad. They had agreed that her hand writing was easier to read than his.

They came up with a long list of things to do and plans for the next five years, at least. Their plans included sports such as basketball, soccer, volleyball, softball, and bowling. They also planned for events such as summer day camp and parties for all ages. They also thought of open gym possibilities.

She wrote up the notes to take to Al. Al would write the final draft before they would take it to the people in charge. This thing was taking off. The wheels were off the ground. But the most difficult tasks were yet to be realized. She was convinced, he seemed that way too. But it hasn't left the gym yet.

It was old home week for her the day they took it to the mission. Al was running things, as usual. She walked around and greeted the volunteers and others who milled about. Some had a crazy look on their faces as they were waiting to be seen. It was almost as if they thought she was trying to cut in line in front of them as they waited to get help. I guess in a way she was.

He spotted the two of them and came right out to greet them. He hugged her like she was his own daughter and gave Rick a firm handshake. That's all he really expected from Al, or even wanted for that matter. It was nothing personal. He just felt more at comfort like that with most men, even his dad.

"So," Al asked, "How did it go?"

"We made a lot of notes," Stacey replied.

"Good, that's the best thing you could've done. What did you come up with?"

That's when Rick entered the conversation.

"We came up with several ways to fix the place up."

"And," Stacey added, "several ideas as well for sports and activities."

"That's great," Al replied, "let's come in and put it all together."

They all walked into his office and sat around his desk.

Al began, "We need three points and a poem. We need to convince, to inspire, and to promote"

She asked, "What about the poem?"

"We'll do what we can."

Rick offered, "I'm glad you're the one writing this thing. I feel like I'm already in over my head."

Al turned on his computer. As they waited for it to give him the opportunity to log on, they made small talk about the weather. Al wanted to dive head first into their thoughts. But they both seemed so nervous. Was this that important to them? He guessed it was.

He seemed to be thinking out loud.

'three points and a poem, convince, inspire, and promote'

She interrupted his thoughts.

"Do we still need a poem?"

"We'll improvise."

He knew that to be something Carol would have provided, poetry.

He read from their notes as he typed the document. She had good handwriting. It proved to be easy to read. And they seemed to function as a team. As he read and wrote, they all talked it over. He wrote a paragraph of introduction, a page to promote the plan, another to convince them of the idea, and he wrapped it all up with an inspirational story.

They were so excited about getting through yet another phase of the plan. Now, Al had to schedule a meeting with a few people before they go to the Association with it. He said he'd let them know when. All they would do now was wait. He kind of encouraged them to use this down time as some time to get to know each other better.

As he watched them walk out the door, he thought better of that last suggestion. Did he speak out of turn? Did he embarrass them? They were nice kids. He thought they'd be good together. They both liked sports and he was under the impression they both jogged. But he was meddling. Isn't that what dads are supposed to do?

They were good together, alright. They got outside and got a football out to play catch. She ran patterns (went out for passes) and he threw her the ball. She caught it and cradled it like she'd been playing forever. She did have a long history of it. She knew the button hook, the post pattern, the flea-flicker, and a few others (like the hail Mary).

Then they talked for hours, made plans for the week...and the weekend, including bowling. But, dinner, Saturday? That was new. That was a date, oh, no. She felt like a school girl again. She agreed to accompany him. He smiled real big, like a school boy. How silly!

When she awoke on Saturday, the realization hit her of what day it was. It was the day she was to go on an actual date with...what's his name? She knew his name. But, would she remember it tonight? Of course, but would he remember hers? What if he forgot where she lived? She giggled at that. He had her number, didn't he?

She went about her day, forgetting her routine. Usually, she stretched, ran ten, worked out, ate a healthy breakfast, showered, changed, and went about her duties for today. But not today. She experienced some confusion. So, she sat down with the word of God and prayed. She needed some clarity.

Then she went about her routine. She had been confused about the gym, Al, Rick, the Association, everything. She wasn't certain of God's plan for her. She didn't know for sure if God was calling her to this. It all seemed so hard, so confusing, like so much work. But it did become clear to her of Rick's part in this.

Speaking of...what's his name, he showed up at seven o'clock, as planned. Wow, he cleaned up real nice. Did she look good enough? He told her she did, the liar. He was nice to say that, though. Oh, now wait, this is a mistake. She couldn't breathe. Why was she so nervous?

They talked over dinner.

"So, Rick, what exactly do you do?"

"I'm involved in project planning for the city, town, area."

"Interesting"

"Yeah, most of my involvement is in implementation. I don't often participate in the planning except for some consultation on electrical work and stuff like that."

"So, do you work on bridges and stuff like that?"

He laughed.

"There is a bridge in the discussion phase right now. It's going to be out at the lake. But I put together electrical transformers and I handle the power at City Hall, the Mayor's office, court house, places like that."

"So, what was funny?"

"Well, it's just that the bridge is supposed to be…hush-hush."

"I'm sorry."

"It's okay, I'm just amazed at your intuitiveness."

"What do you mean?"

"Well, that was supposed to be a secret."

After dinner, they went to the city to see a movie. In the dark, she began to realize she was on a date. Perhaps that was due to the fact that they were in a dark place, sitting side by side. What do grown-ups do about holding hands? Don't look around to find out. Don't…look! It's all on him.

He held her hand at the movie. She liked it. She sat in the middle of his seat in the pick-up. This was a date and she liked it. Would he try to kiss her good-night? Would she allow it? Would she want him to? Ah, who cares? She enjoyed his company. Oh, what, is he talking? She had been day dreaming. She was acting just like her eighth grade self again.

He dropped her off. He walked her to the door. He said good-night. And then he stood there, as did she. The suspense was enthralling. She was ready. Was he? Maybe she wasn't ready. He finally said good-night and saw her into her door before leaving. He did, however, promise to call.

She was glad that he didn't. They weren't ready. She prayed, though. She was thankful for him, his friendship, all he had done and will do. The stress that had been there before was at the present relieved. She now knew where she stood with him and with herself. And soon she would know where she stood with her job here. Is *that* what was affecting her so much?

2

For a year, she had been uncertain where she stood with Al and the mission. Every day she was shut up in that little room filling out reports and requisitions, wondering if she was in the right place. And then Al takes her to the gym and her worries are over. That is, until she finds she has to face this review board, and speak.

She knew she wasn't called to preach, maybe teach, but not preach. That knowledge had always been good to have because she was terrified of speaking in public. She'd rather die. And, according to statistics, so would anybody. Death was only number two on the all- time fear list.

Al spotted her on Sunday. Rick still went to another church. But she sat among this congregation, never to lead it, never to want to.

"Stacey, I've got news. We're meeting a week from tomorrow with a few people from the Association. Tom will be there. You met him."

"Yeah, ..."

"The Association Rec guy will also be there as well as the pastor of First Church. I think they can be a real asset here."

"Okay..."

"Can you let Rick know? I'd like the three of us to present."

There it was, the call to speak in front of people.

"Yeah, I can do that. When, a week from Monday, you said?"

"Yes, next Monday. Are you okay?"

"Yeah, it's just that speaking in public, is not easy for me."

"Don't I know?"

That surprised her. He spoke in public every Sunday.

"Yeah, I preach here every Sunday…"

'Did he hear me say that,' she wondered.

"…but these people are funny."

That didn't seem relevant because these three aforementioned people weren't family. Or, were they?

"Three men, you say?"

"You're used to that, aren't you?"

He was speaking of their bowling trio.

"Yeah, a dad and two big brothers."

She felt so confident all of a sudden. This was going to be like a Sunday dinner. All of the guys will sit around and talk. And she would contribute to the conversation. Yeah, this will old home week for her. She couldn't wait until that second Monday from now. All she had to do was call… Rick.

As she began to dial, it occurred to her what day it was. Yes, it was Sunday. But, it's also the day…aft-er…the date! No, put it away. She can't call him the day after…Is there a teenage girl in the room? No, it's her. But this isn't date related. Oh, no, there are date related things? How exactly did that happen? But, he does need to know. Then something startled her. It was her phone ringing. It was him. He was calling the day after. What was wrong with him? Didn't anybody explain the rules of dating…Wait a minute, dating?

"Hello, Rick."

"Stacey, hi, how are you?"

"I'm fine, you?"

"I'm doing pretty well. Did you enjoy yourself last night?"

"I did. Thanks again."

"Sure, well, I just called to check on you. I guess I'll…"

"A week from tomorrow, Rick."

"What?"

"Uh, we're meeting with Al and some people about the gym."

"Oh, okay, thanks!"

That was a silly phone call. So, why was she still smiling, and laughing a little? She didn't know...it didn't matter. That call meant only one thing: that she wouldn't have to sit around waiting for it. When would he call again? He wouldn't. They would just meet up again for the meeting. If he came by to pick her, she would have left already.

It was Wednesday. He called last night. He inquired of her plans for Saturday and if she were going bowling on Friday. Yes, she had made plans to go on Friday. But, he needed to understand that she just wanted to be friends. She agreed to Saturday only for the purpose of giving him...the speech.

On Friday, Al didn't mention the upcoming meeting. She got nervous about that. But, then again, maybe that's why he didn't talk about it, so that he wouldn't make her nervous. Maybe something was wrong. Did the earth open up underneath them? They were in the abyss and he didn't tell her. But, wait, if...

She rehearsed her speech all day Saturday. Al did, by the way, remind them last night of the upcoming meeting. But, that's all he said. She was distracted by...both situations. It's a good thing she's young. She had too much on her mind. She prayed and went on a run. That, once again, proved to clear her head.

She ate a brunch, all healthy food. She cleaned up and felt refreshed as she lay down for a nap. She dreamed about little kids playing soccer, grown-ups in a basketball league, softball, and football. Football was her absolute favorite sport. Is that why she's dating a quarterback? No! They're not dating. Quit saying that!

She woke up and cleaned up for...date, she guessed. She must have that talk with him. You know, the friends talk. It might disappoint, or maybe hurt him. She felt sorry for the poor fellow. She almost began to cry. It was his own fault for pursuing her. She smiled at that idea, his pursuit of her.

She watched him pull into her driveway. She pitied the foolish guy. He pulled in here, probably expecting more than she was willing to give. It wasn't sexual. It was emotional and, yes spiritual. But she couldn't have it. She liked him. She really liked him…no, get out of that!

She greeted him at the door.

"Rick, hi."

"Hi, Stacey, ready?"

"Yeah, let's go."

"Hey, I thought we'd go somewhere and… talk."

Talk, about what?

They rode to the restaurant in silence. She wondered if he were going to give her the speech. I mean, what difference will it make? Isn't that what she was going to do? So, why did it bother her? Oh, well, at least she gets a meal out of it. Should she try to beat him to it? This wasn't a competition.

They found a nice, cozy table. He seemed to want to be away from others. He pulled her chair out, typical. Just before he drops the 'friends bomb', he treats her like a lady. He sat down across from her. They ordered their drinks. There was some small talk. Then the waitress took their dinner order. And that's when the 'talk' began.

"Stacey," he began as he crossed his hands in front of him.

"Yeah, Rick, what's up?"

Was she kidding?

"What? Never mind. Stacey, tomorrow, I'm going to meet with Al after church for lunch. You're more than welcome. I want to talk about Monday."

"Oh, okay. Yeah, I'll be there."

"I was hoping you and I could talk about it tonight."

"Yeah, sure, let's."

"Great, now,…"

They discussed about how they felt about this meeting and how they wanted to approach it. It was important to be on the same page. And the next day they would have one last planning meeting before they met with the three on Monday. Al was having lunch catered in that day from the cafeteria.

He drove her home and she felt good about tonight. He hadn't really said anything…personal. He talked about his dad and Al and the gym. She wondered if there was a 'them'. She felt it for her part. But, what about him? He did hold her hand last time. What would he do this time? Somehow, it just didn't seem to matter anymore.

He got her home and he said he looked forward to seeing her tomorrow. She felt good about him. He didn't seem to expect anything from her, not even a good-night kiss. She felt good about him. He didn't seem to expect anything from her, not even a good-night kiss. She felt good, about herself, around him, though. He was comfortable to be around. He's a real nice guy. She could see herself as a friend of his.

They went to church together Sunday at the mission. They even sat together. Al spotted them both and greeted them before the service. He said he would take them out to lunch at a local diner and they could discuss their game plan. They sat through the service. Al on serving God by serving others, the widows, the orphans, the Samaritans, etc…

After the service, Al kept his word and drove them out to a diner. It was his same old haunt. So, everybody said hi and greeted the kids with him. There were lots of speculations as to who they might be. It didn't seem to be his daughter, so they didn't know who either of them were. But some did recognize them.

Rick waved hello to a few of them that he knew, some from work. Stacey remembered one or two from the time before when Al had brought her here before. As they sat down, the waitress anticipated his order of a cup of coffee before his meal. She asked for water and Rick ordered a glass of root beer. Al, not to the surprise of the waitress, indicated it was all on his tab.

"Well, you two, here's how it's going to go down tomorrow…
Real serious now.

"We're all meeting at the center for lunch at noon…

High noon.

"Then we're going into the conference room...

The waitress brought over their drinks and took their food orders. She remembered how Stacey had eaten like a bird. But Rick and Al both made up for it.

"Anyway," he continued, "I'll begin and I'll introduce you...

Pointing at her "Rick, I think it would be helpful if you said a thing or two about what you are doing to fix things, like electrical, plumbing, construction, etc..."

Rick looked surprised, though he really wasn't.

"Sure thing," he answered.

"Great, thanks. Realize here, it'll be like preaching to the choir with these three. So, don't be nervous. They're already on our side, but we need to bring them up to speed."

Their dinners arrived and they ate in pleasant conversation. Al wanted to find out about them. He was concerned, curious, nosy.

Al's daughter had met her husband in college. So, by the time Al me him, they were already an item. He almost never had any involvement in her life. He had always been so busy. His wife was very involved, however, although she also involved in his job at the mission.

Al paid the check and drove them back to the mission. After they said good-bye, he watched as they climbed into Rick's truck. She sat in the middle of seat. He knew what that meant. He felt privileged to witness the evolution of budding romance. One day, they might get married and have children. And he could say he witnessed the whole thing as it metamorphasized.

Rick drove her home. It was such a pleasant day for a drive, for anything really. They both felt as ease as they talked about what Al said about these three guys. They knew he was right. Convincing these guys wasn't even necessary. And after it was over, there will be six of them. Their numbers would double and they would need that.

She relaxed the rest of the day. She prayed, thanking God for Al...and Rick. She was thankful for him but it felt so weird admitting it. But most of all, she was thankful that it was going to be so easy to talk to these guys. She could use the practice. Who knows that someday she would have to do this again (shudder.)

She went straight to the gym on Monday morning. She had made plans to meet Rick at the mission. Those plans were kind of his idea. He was keeping this thing a nothing for some reason. Maybe he didn't like her at all. No, he likes her. She could tell in other ways. There were just some things he said and did.

She ran. She stretched. She worked out. She showered and dressed. What a morning. What a job. She looked at it now and imagined it in the future. She couldn't wait. It all belonged to God. He would make this happen. She just felt like it was right. So, what was she worried about?

Rick pulled into the parking lot right behind her. She was kind of relieved he showed up. She had though, for a second (or more) that he might not show at all. She was afraid, for some reason, that he would disappoint her. But this meeting wasn't the one that she really depended on him for. Oh, did his showing up for this one that he wouldn't be there for the important one?

They walked in together and both took a deep breath before proceeding to the cafeteria for lunch. She wasn't hungry. But, apparently, he was. He did, however, step aside to allow her to enter first. Whatever, she thought. But it was certainly nice of him. Of course, that meant that he would follow her in. She was in the lead now.

This also meant that she would be in line at the cafeteria in front of him. She got first choice in front of him. It reminded her of her brothers. But they never allowed her to be in front of them. Instead, they placed her behind them because they always believed the older siblings should receive first dibs on everything. She disagreed but they didn't care.

She looked for Al when she got ready to sit down. He sat at a round table with about eight chairs. She guessed he expected their guests to eat there with them. It was a decent lunch today. Would they see fit to eat there? Or, would they eat on the way? Rick nudged her in Al's direction. Pushy much?

They joined Al at the table. She asked if the three would be joining them for lunch. He said he wasn't certain but he got a table big enough just in case. She thought that that made perfect sense. Al had been doing things for a long time now. He was in charge today and she felt very comfortable there. He was strong, like her father.

The pastor joined them a few minutes later. Tom was ten minutes later as he announced that the rec guy was eating somewhere else but that he would be there at one o'clock for the meeting. So, they had a nice lunch. Stacey liked the pastor. He was also a good leader. Tom was kind of a beaurocrat but he seemed to know what he was doing.

He did show up for the meeting. He met them all in the hallway. She was becoming excited (not about him) and nervous, scared, elated, all of it, all at once. She didn't even care that she was the only female present. As a matter of fact, she liked it that way. She felt a bit intimidated but that served only to challenge her.

They entered the conference room and all the appropriate introductions were made. Most everybody already knew each other. Tom and the rec guy had been there at the Association office for her hiring. She had met the pastor before. Rick got introduced but of course Al knew everybody present. That's why he spoke first.

"Ladies, Stacey, and gentlemen," he began.

"I do appreciate all of you coming out today.

He motioned toward the three.

"Gentlemen, I have requested your presence today to discuss a proposal for reopening the Association gym. Eight years ago, it was closed due to safety concerns regarding a mechanical failure with one of the cranks that operate the basketball goals. But…He now motioned toward Rick.

"This young man, a Civil Engineer has already repaired that particular problem.

"He has also managed to perform inspections on the electrical, the plumbing, the paint, etc…

"But, more relevant, I think…

He checked with Rick, who gave a nod of agreement.

"…is the young woman of whom I have no doubt that she is actually qualified to run the gym. Gentlemen, please allow me to introduce Stacey. She comes to us here from seminary with a degree in church recreation."

Both Tom and the rec director gave knowing nods of her qualifications. The pastor seemed rightfully impressed.

She confirmed his nod.

She giggled, involuntarily of course, as The three looked at each other self-consciously.

"I'm sorry," she began, "it's just that, as I speak, I am picturing my father, brothers, and other male members of my family. Please understand, my father is retired Navy and my brothers both played football. So, you see, I grew up around men.

They smiled. The pastor chuckled, as did Al and Rick.

"Anyway, it is true that I received a seminary degree in church rec. And, throughout seminary, I worked for a church as manager of their skate program with kids on Wednesday evenings.

"I did my internship at a church camp. We did water sports there. It's strange, but although my father was a Navy officer, I wasn't familiar with water sports. But it was a wonderful, learning experience for me.

"But, as far as the gym is concerned, it was love at first sight when I saw that gym. Even with the broken goal, I knew that was the place for me. And then Al showed me the room with all the sports equipment, with the electronic air pump. Finally, I felt like I was finally where I belonged.

"My plans include basketball leagues for both adults and children, a children's soccer league, adult softball and bowling. And, finally, sometime in the future I'd like to coach volleyball and conduct day camps."

"Excuse me, Stacey," came the rec director from the Association.

"Can you tell us more about these, uh, day camps and when you might estimate getting started.

"Yes, certainly, the day camps will be those Bible clubs they do in the summer, only I'd like to personally conduct them, with help from a team from the college, in the summer. But that won't happen, probably until next year.

"In this current year, I hope to spend the time in renovation of the gym. But, hopefully, next year I will be able to conduct basketball in the winter, softball in the spring, perhaps a soccer clinic in the summer and bowling in the fall.

"But, around mid-October, I'd like to begin to open our doors for holiday events until after the first of the year.

"And, as I mentioned earlier, I would someday hope to coach volleyball and hold day camps.

"But, as far as fixing the maintenance issues, I'll leave those to the expert."

She glanced at Rick. He took that as his cue.

"Yes, gentlemen," he began, "I have already repaired the basketball goal.

"My next project will be the electrical. I'll probably overhaul the power box. And, I will replace most of the water pipes. Finally, I'll bring in a crew to paint the wall up by the ceiling. And, at some point in the future, we'll bring in roofers."

Everyone seemed overwhelmed by all of that. It seemed like a lot to do. But her ideas were great.

"Well," Tom began, "it all sounds great. But there seems to be a lot of repair work to do."

The rec guy interrupted. "That's just because it was allowed to remain closed for so long. I feel like it will all be worth it."

Tom spoke again.

"I agree that Stacey has good ideas. And I feel like it's worth the money and effort. I'm just saying that it won't be easy to convince the rest of the Association to put that money out.

Al knew that asking for the money would be like pulling teeth.

"I'll get back to you with a time to bring it in to them.

He stood to leave and shook their hands.

"You have my support."

"And mine as well," said the rec guy.

They left and the pastor approached Al.

"Al had you made plans to speak to the Association?"

"I'm pretty certain I will."

"I mean, preach?"

"No, why?"

"If you don't mind, I'd like to bring the Word."

"Sounds divine!"

"I don't know about that. But I was just thinking about recreation. It's re-creation, re-creating ourselves. I think I can put something together for that."

They agreed and the pastor hugged her and shook Rick's hand as he left, excited to be a part of this.

Al began to speak to the two of them.

"I'll be sure and let you'll know about the meeting."

"You think it went all right?" Rick asked.

Al answered, "It went great. Although, for a second, I thought you were going to talk them out of it."

"Sorry!" embarrassed.

"Oh, no, it's okay. I mean, they needed to hear that. And, the rec guy was right."

"James", Stacey said.

"Excuse me?"

"His name is James. I remember from the interview."

"Thanks, I keep forgetting. I'm really terrible with names."

Rick and Stacey left. She returned to the gym and he returned to work. Al finished the rest of the day mopping up day to day tasks. All three went away feeling encouraged. She mussed about the gym. She organized the equipment room. She swept and dry mopped the gym floor. She also got busy and cleaned up some mildew from the showers.

3

Instead of Al calling her, Tom called her. He told her they had a meeting set for a week away. It was Thursday. Her heart sank. She was scared. What was she thinking? She simply couldn't go through with it. But it would be worth it if it actually got approved. What a big if. They turned from preaching to the choir back to the real people.

Rick called on Friday. She told him about the meeting. He asked her if she was ready. She wanted to say no. She wanted to cancel the whole thing. But she couldn't make that decision for the both of them. He deserved to come or go, fight or flight, stay or betray.

On Sunday evening, she put in a call to her dad. She felt like she needed to hear his voice. She hadn't talked to him in a while. He never had approved of her having taken that job there. He had said that he thought that she should have stayed home and taught children, maybe coach some girls' soccer or something. But, wasn't there something in his life that influenced her to reach beyond her comfort zone (military?) Maybe he had just feared losing her.

"Hello!" came his voice on the other end.

"Dad? This is Stacey."

"My darling little wanderer.

'Not anymore' she thought.

"Long time, no hear."

"Yeah, sorry, I've been busy."

"What'cha doin'?"

"I'm kind of in the middle of something rather important right now."

"Oh, what kind of something?"

"We're renovating a gymnasium for the purpose of recreational activity."

"So, what are you doing?"

"I'm in charge of the gym."

She thought he might actually be proud, but…

"In charge, of who?"

"…of everyone who uses the gym."

"Certainly not the men, I would hope."

"everyone, Dad"

"I just don't understand how…I mean, I thought that the church…how is that?"

"How is what?"

"You know, that you would be…in charge…of men…since you're, you know…"

"a girl, Dad?"

"Don't get me wrong. I just…

'You just think I'm still my brothers' little sister.'

"Well, what are you doing?"

"What do you mean?"

"…well, with this project you're doing."

"I have to convince some people to spend the money for it."

"What people?"

"…church association people."

"Is that kind of like a Senate Appropriations Committee?"

"…well, kind of, but not that…uh…important…I guess."

"But, why you?"

"They want to hear from me because…

She wasn't about to say it again.

"Anyway, it's this Thursday, and…"

"Why don't you just forget about it and come home?"

"And do what?"

"You can teach children and coach...girls..."

"No, Dad, I'm staying here. I just hoped you'd give me some encouragement."

He changed the topic.

"Your oldest brother is in town. You think you can make it down here to see him?"

She'd like to.

"Not this time, sorry."

"Why are you avoiding your own family, your brothers?"

Was he calling her ambitious?

"I'm not avoiding them. I'm just (sigh) busy right now."

"You should never be too busy for family."

She wanted to explode. How many tours did he volunteer for? One day, she would confront him on that. But, not now, not over the phone.

"I'm going to get off the phone now, Dad."

"I'll break the news to your brother."

They said their 'I love you's' and bid each other good-night. She was not encouraged. Her enthusiasm was swallowed up in depression. She felt like going to Al and calling the whole thing off. But Al and Rick had both put so much into this already. She felt caught in the middle. She can't quit now, but she wants to.

She went to the mission the next day. She wanted to talk to Al regarding her feeling of discouragement. She was ready to tell him it was over and done. But she just couldn't do that to him and Rick. She didn't know what to do. She kept shaking her head as she thought about it. There was just no way. They would have to drag her through it. It was the only way.

But, who's that? She saw an adolescent female, sitting, brooding, arms crossed, pouty face.

It was Bob and Alice's daughter. She had met her before. She approached her.

"What's going on?"

"Boys, they won't let me play football. My dad says…

Stacey tried, unsuccessfully, to quail a laugh.

"It's not funny!"

"I'm sorry. It's just, when I was your age, I wanted to play football. But, my dad, well, you obviously know…"

"What did you do?"

She couldn't encourage her with good news that she played anyway.

"I played soccer, basketball, and volleyball. And I bowled."

"I like bowling."

"You like soccer?"

"Yeah, that's fun!"

"Well, if everything goes well, I'll be coaching soccer soon."

"Cool, when, where, how do I get started?"

"I'll let you know."

Suddenly, she rose on fire again. She had almost forgotten why she was doing this. She had become so wrapped up in self-pity, just like when she was that girl's age. Her father had, once again, taken her back to that time. He said she can't play with boys at a man's game. Oh, Daddy!

Al saw her and greeted her. He asked her if she were there for the strategy meeting. Had Tom mentioned that and she forgot? She just said yes. Rick was there. He said he'd gone to pick her up but she wasn't there. He was worried.

'Oh, really?'

She didn't bother to mention the real reason she had come in this morning, to quit.

It did seem strange, however, that that young girl had been there, right at that moment. She didn't question it, however. No, she just accepted it as the right thing at the right moment. She was thankful for it, for her. It was a God thing for sure. Her whole calling was a God thing. How did He call her out of that life to what He did call her to?

The six of them discussed how they would proceed this coming Thursday. Tom assumed command of this particular meeting. He knew the individuals they would be up against. He was entirely in favor of the pastor of First Church preaching at the meeting. And he offered speaking pointers to Rick and Stacey. He request of Rick a cost analysis and of Stacey a timetable of upcoming events.

Rick was accustomed to the concept of a cost analysis. He had been involved in a few on projects in his occupation. And Tom had confidence in Al's ability to assist Stacey with the time projection table. He said he'd edit them if they so desired but only to the end of making minor changes. Otherwise, he said he would see them all on Thursday at the Association office.

Tuesday, she ran laps in the gym. She crossed those up with wind sprints (suicides). She ran hard and fast. She thought about her father, the Association, that girl. She also thought about Rick. She didn't understand what was keeping him away from her. Did he like her or not? She finally stopped, both thinking and running.

Rick invited her to his church for Wednesday night Bible study. She agreed. She thought that that's what she needed more of, communal Bible study. She read her Bible, but she felt like she needed both the input and perspective of others to help her grow in it. Besides, she felt also the need for what was to come the following day. And, guess who else went to that church, Bob and Alice. She always liked them.

Her and Rick talked for hours that night. Rick said he had something to do at work before he could get away. But, he would be there. She wanted to DTR (define the relationship) but something inside of her told her to wait it out. He likes you, girl! She liked him. And, what if he DTR'd? He had better not! No, girl, just enjoy this time you have.

Sleep did not come easy to her that night. She thought a lot about being daddy's girl. He would not even notice what she did there. She couldn't, she wouldn't so much as invite him because he would not offer any support. Her mom's death was hard on both of them. That's something they had in common, perhaps the only thing.

Obviously, she did manage some sleep because her alarm awoke her in the middle of a dream. She woke up tired and queasy. Her usual brand breakfast just wouldn't do today. She needed more but, at the same time, she didn't want to be weighed down today. Okay, bran it is.

Her and Al had put the plan together Wednesday morning. It was when Rick came in to ask Al to check his work that he invited her to church. The time table actually appeared more like a set of three calendars: a daily planner, a weekly planner, and a monthly, with an over-all projection for the entire year. She was impressed with Al's understanding of his calendar software.

She wrestled with decisions regarding apparel for the day. Should she wear a suit, tie, maybe a skirt, blouse, what color? Should she call Rick to see what…no, wait, girls do that. Besides, he had to go to work first. So, he'll be in work clothes. Oh, wait a minute. She knew just what to wear. Of course, it would represent just what she was doing.

She pulled into the parking lot sporting a designer sweat suit (jogging outfit). She had never run in it (or anything else in it). She figured it was appropriate, as she was trying to open a gymnasium. Not to mention it was comfortable and casual. Perhaps, it was too casual. Oh, no, did she make an error in judgment? It's too late now, anyway.

"You look perfect for the part," Tom said as he greeted her at the door.

"Thank you!"

He was in a suit, but that's his style.

"I was concerned that you would get all dressed up for it. I really should have given you a heads up."

Rick arrived shortly thereafter. Yeah, she was right, he had on his work clothes. It brought a smile to her face. He sidled up to her and Tom. They shook hands and she hugged him. He was all smiles himself at that. They both had their presentations ready. She told Tom Al had helped her with it. That was good enough for him.

And then walked in Al and the pastor. They made a jolly entrance together, a couple of preachers. They wore suits and smiles. Boy, were she and Rick underdressed. They all greeted one another with hugs and hand shakes. The two preachers joked about this and that. She didn't see James. Tom said he'd arrive with the others.

It kind of seemed to her that Tom and James were drifting. She hoped, she wondered if they were still there for them. Suddenly, she felt like a mouse caught in a trap. She was a cornered animal. And she heard her father's dismissal of her purposes and her calling. Al and the pastor didn't seem worried. Neither did Rick.

They proceeded to a large conference room. There was a large table with about twelve chairs, two on each end five on each side. A smaller table was set to the side with juice, bagels (white, oh well), jellies, and water (with cups). She ate a plain bagel and drank some juice.

Tom sat at one end of the table. He directed them around to different places at the table. She was surprised Al didn't sit on the other end. But, then again, he's done this before. So, he knows what to do and where to sit. Al sat on one side close to Tom. The pastor sat one the other side on the other end. She placed herself next to him and Rick sat across from her.

James arrived with six others. They didn't have them outnumbered. It was a game. The seating was strategic. Al and Tom represented a united front. And, since Al and the pastor were to bring the inspiration, they chose to do so in stereo. Her and Rick would volley off of each other. And they sat first so the board members would be forced to accept whatever seats remained.

James had met his personal obligations by getting them to arrive a few minutes after they had. Well, he was still a member of their team. Tom had produced copies of the Time Table and Cost

Analysis. So, he had two stacks of paperwork in front of him. And on the other end of the table sat Abigail. She was tall, thin, and spectacled. But, she also brought in paperwork.

Tom made introductions as everyone sat with their bagels, jelly, cream cheese, and juice or water. James had come in wearing what appeared to be an outfit for a tennis pro. Just as with her, appropriate. But, everybody else sported suits. James didn't appear concerned. As a matter of fact, he and Abigail had each brought their own water containers.

Tom began, "Ladies and Gentlemen, thank you for your attention to this matter today. I have requested your participation…

'That's right' she thought, 'Tom is in charge of these particular people.'

"…in this discussion regarding the reopening of the old gymnasium under the direction of mission staff.

'Oh, that would be her.'

"I have called on some people to talk with all of you on the board regarding this matter, including their vision for the mission and the Association.

"Allow me to present you with some background. Approximately eight years ago, the Association gym was closed due to a mechanical failure involving a basketball goal having been mistakenly locked into position. The gym was condemned due to a fear that the goal would come crashing down, causing injury or death.

'…or a class action suit' Al thought.

"There is, however, a gym at First Church, but it's only open to members, which doesn't do the rest of us in the Association any good.

'…good one!'

"One of the presenters for today is Stacey. She possesses a seminary degree inchurch recreation and she has experience in that field. James and I hired her about a year ago and she has proved to be valuable.

"Rick is a home town fellow, born and raised. However, he

went away from us for six years and obtained a Masters Degree in engineering. He returned to us a few years ago upon accepting a job with the city as Civil Engineer. Rick has been instrumental in the Bridge Project along with a few structures in town and the irrigation system as well.

"However, before we hear from the two of them, I have requested of Reverend Al Bryant, director of the Associational Mission Center, to share his perspective. Stacey works with Al, so I'd like him to share with you all that he knows about Stacey and the gym as well as his connection to Rick.

"Al?"

"Thanks, Tom.

"What I have to say, well, is a little embarrassing. It seems that the first impression I had of Stacey was negative, but not on her point or mine. She has done everything right. Whereas, I've made some poor choices, such as my relegation of her to paperwork.

"However, I find myself inspired by her work and her enthusiasm. We were in need of a Rec Director and now we have one.

"I've known Rick for a long time now. His father is not only my friend, he's my physician. I happen to know of his father's pride in all he has managed to accomplish.

She looked across and Rick was smiling.

"They make a good pair.

That struck her as a tad personal.

"I mean…a good team.

"But I believe that Stacey has some paperwork she'd like to share with you regarding her plans and goals."

She froze. She had the Time Table right in front of her. But suddenly, it seemed useless, futile. She heard echoes of her father talking about just how much of a waste of time this was. But she was also afraid that her measly efforts would prove to have been a waste of time for Al and Rick.

She knew neither what to say or how to say it.

Then Tom said, "Stacey, may I see one of those time tables?"

He told on himself. He wasn't supposed to know what it was.

"Yes, here you go." She began.

She passed them around the table.

She continued, "What I have prepared for you today is a time table of events.

"As you can see, from the present until summer of next year, we will be working toward preparing the gym (pending approval). I shall conduct soccer, day camps for children.

'What a great idea!' she thought.

"In the fall is bowling for adults and children, with basketball in the winter...for both.

"But, in the in, between, will be holiday celebrations, such as the Harvest Festival...

She peered at what might or might not have been expectant ears...waiting for the word...Halloween.

"...Thanksgiving, Christmas, and New Years. And, finally, in the spring will be softball...for adults.

She almost forgot.

"One day, though, I would like teaching...coaching volleyball as well.

"Thank you."

Al nodded in a fatherly approval sort of way.

Then he introduced Rick.

Rick passed his cost analysis sheets around. She thought that his would prove more difficult to present than was hers. She was so thankful he was the one of the two of them presenting this one.

He began, "I just wanted to begin by thanking you all for your thoughtful consideration.

His speech was eloquent and confidant. He didn't bat an eye lash. She was so impressed that she only heard half of what he said.

"And that's what I see as the cost for this particular project.

"Thank you all."

"Thanks, Rick," Tom replied.

Then, "And, finally, the pastor of First Church would like to bring a word. Pastor…"

"Thank you, Tom."

He spoke of recreation being a re-creation. He related it to the rebirth that we experience with Christ as Christians. He then spoke of exercise as a positive activity in our regrouping and how we exercise our faith like we exercise our bodies, to make it stronger like we make our body stronger. He used the analogy of no pain, no gain to talk about breaking down and building up our faith like we do our bodies.

It was awesome! The message was very clear and dramatic. He sure had a flare for it. As a matter of fact, everybody was on the same side afterward. There remained no more reason to feel nervous. Everybody was on the same page now. Everyone got so friendly afterward. They were all like old friends… now.

But, they still had to process it a little more. There was a procedure to follow. There were other people to talk to. But certain people such as those at First Church who had wanted everyone to know that they had the only gym in the Association, were not in that certain of need-to-know. So, now all they could do was wait. Tom said he would be in touch.

4

The waiting period proved to be a little longer than what was originally anticipated. Days turned into weeks until a couple of months had passed. Her and Rick did some work around the gym. She even began planning for sports. She performed the job she had been hired to do. She didn't allow anything to interrupt her groove.

One evening, though, she received a phone call.

"Hello."

"Stacey?"

"Aunt Claire?!"

Her dad's sister.

"Yes, dear, how are you?"

"I'm fine. Wow, it's so awesome for you to call."

"Well, dear, I'm calling because my dear brother called me, accusing me of putting ideas in your head."

"Ideas, about what?"

"...about having a career, a degree..."

She fumed!

"...all kinds of things he thinks I put you up to."

"I am so sorry. I'll talk..."

"No, dear, don't be sorry. It was just another good excuse to tell him off."

"Oh?"

"Oh, don't worry. I didn't hurt the big lug. I just reminded him of who it is that you really take after…"

(Silence. Sadness.)

Then "Mom."

"Well, a little bit like me, but, yeah, your mom."

(Laughter)

"Little girl, your daddy is a big, rough, tough Naval officer. But, when it comes to his little girl, he's a frightened rabbit."

"Frightened, of what?"

"…of losing you, like he lost her."

They talked for a little while. She felt sorry for him. She mentioned something about talking with her brother Billy, the middle child. He misses his mom. But older brother Bobby is strong and stubborn like Dad. Stacey merely smiled and nodded at that information that she knew already.

Finally, one Monday, Al called her in to tell her of the decision made by the board. They had made a few visits, one unexpected, to the gym. They had looked at every nook and cranny. It worried her but Rick just took notes. Al said they had done the same at the mission.

Rick showed up to give her a ride to the mission. She didn't, however, need a ride because she had a car. But, he did come all this way. Besides, he always seemed to feel obligated to take her to lunch when he was driving. And, she wanted this opportunity to tell him about her conversation with her aunt. She also had decided that, no matter what, she would call her dad afterward.

She did tell him all about it. He chuckled about her aunt. But, he understood about her dad. He had lost his mom as well. But, he had been in Middle school at the time, not away at college. And he lost his lost his mom to a horseback incident. He was about fourteen when it happened. They, indeed, had something in common.

They arrived at the mission and walked straight to Al's office. She hadn't noticed, but she had left Rick behind. He chuckled again and followed obediently. Al, being the gentleman, stood as she walked in, forgetting to knock. Unfortunately, she realized what she had done. She had left Rick behind and forgot to knock on Al's door before entering. He just motioned her to a chair.

Rick peeked into the already open door and was welcomed as well. He sat next to her. He took her hand and she smiled her approval. Al nodded at the scene. Then he sat down and pulled out a file folder full of paper. He handed it to her and she sported a look of utter confusion.

He told her to open it and Rick peered upon it as well. The first page was a cover letter, explaining the intent of the Association, alongside Stacey, Rick, and Al to renovate the mission gym for the purpose of reopening to the public for use as directed by...her name. Her eyes almost fell out of her head.

'Directed by me, little ole me?' she thought.

The rest of it was her time line and his cost analysis with a few proposed addendums. But, the last page required her signature for approval of the proposal changes. She liked it. She liked it all. She signed it and this was her job now. She had fallen right into this position. And she loved it! She loved it all!

They ate lunch at the mission. But, Rick took her out to dinner that evening, as promised. They had a lot of work ahead of them to do. She was looking forward to it. It was right up her alley. She was fulfilling her mission now. All of those years of school were, finally, being put to the use that they were made for.

He picked her up around seven. She was happy. She was prepared for anything. Rick couldn't help but smile as he saw her in her short dress. He remarked of how lovely she was. She thanked him and floated to his truck. Nothing could bother her tonight. He suggested dinner and a movie. She approved with vigor.

Dinner was at a nice place. Tonight, he showed her how much money he made. He also showed her how much she was worth spending on. They had steaks and salads, not to mention conversation. But, that was very intimate and personal. This guy would, she thought, fit in real well with the men in her family.

He could throw, or try to throw, a touchdown pass to Billy before Bobby (ouch) crushed his bones. She giggled. He asked what it was that he said that was so funny. She responded that she was picturing him playing football with her brothers. He said she could play too. She said,

"Really?!"

He responded, "really!"

She smiled and felt good about his company tonight.

She didn't really get into chick flicks as much as one might think. She actually liked sports movies. She felt like the 'chics' were weak and vulnerable. Their gray matter seemed to just…fade as the movies progressed. It was like she was saying,

"Okay, fine, I'll kiss him. Just get this mess over with already."

He didn't hold her hand this time. Instead, he put his arm around her. And, he didn't (fake) yawn first. He just did it. And she just allowed it. It was all so natural. The movie was an inspirational movie about a Christian school football team that overcomes all odds to win a championship.

The drive to her place was full of chatter. She told him what she had been giggling about before, her big brother trying to catch him so that he could 'DT' him with a linebacker style body slam. Rick somehow failed to see the humor. She mentioned that it was okay because Rick could outrun him. He inquired of her certainty of that fact. She said, yes, he could, and she would block for him.

He walked her to the door. He put off saying good-night. After a minute, she figured out why. He said he'd been holding out for the end of all this business with the Association. He said he really cared for her. She said she did as well. Things got pretty serious, pretty intimate, before…the kiss. It was nice.

So, that's what he was waiting for. He finally said good-night and went on his way. She wanted to tell somebody. But, who? She knew a few women, but they weren't that kind of friend, none of them. She wished she could tell her mom. If only she had a sister. So, she decided to tell her aunt.

Wow, she's got a boyfriend. What to do with him, that's the question. She already had him using his many skills to assist her at the gym. She could play catch with him. But, would they get married? Playing catch could lead to that if he put an engagement ring on the ball and throw it to her. Or, if he got on one knee after a rousing game of catch.

Her aunt gave her kudos over having been kissed by a handsome man. Then she called her dad. She wanted to listen to him again, but this time she wanted to hear the love in his voice. She wanted to hear his concern for her, his fear of losing her like he did her mom, like they did. She wanted to talk with him about that. But she didn't know how.

She went to work and the work began for her right away. She had to do everything just right in order to get the gym ready. She never feared that it would not happen because it had seemed right. She sensed that she was in God's will with the gym, and with Rick. He worked really hard there. But she felt like he was doing it all for her. That...was okay.

They worked tirelessly through the summer. Volunteers showed up to help every day. Al frequented several times a week. Then one day they sent him a new assistant to replace her as she was now working full time in the gym. This time it was a man to serve as Associate Pastor. He removed a lot of the burden off of Al.

Sadly, though, the pastor of First Church accepted a job somewhere else. Another church in the Association closed over a split. The Rec Director at the Association accepted a position with the National Mission Board. This didn't all take place over the summer. It was spread out over the next year. Lots of changes affected a lot of lives that year.

In the fall, Al conducted his revival with a team from the college. And they held the Harvest Party, at the mission because the gym wasn't quite ready. But, Al announced to everyone that next year it would be held at the gym. She wanted to be happy but she was too tired. She worked hard at this.

Al's new assistant's name was Gabe Hurle. He was in his forties and possessed experience in pastoring and preaching. Al appeared tired...and sad. Some people from the mission and around the Association had passed. Sadly, his lawyer friend from the bowling alley had passed as well. Al seemed sort of distant, relieved to have help. He also seemed to be a bit preoccupied at times.

Al's friend had passed during the winter. They had the Harvest Party and served Thanksgiving dinner. Alice was always such a big help with that. And, now, her daughter was pitching in to help as well. Lots of women, and Aaron Wilson as well, helped at both Thanksgiving and Christmas. New Year's was literally a blast with the fireworks.

Al and his assistant both taught discipleship classes in January and February. Stacey spent some time with her new, young female companion, throwing the football around. Also, she and Rick spent a lot of time together. She seemed to spend less time working in the gym during this time.

However, she came out of hiding in the spring time and returned to her work in the gym. She had spent a couple of weeks back home. Her dad attempted to talk (guilt) her into actually, of all things, moving back home. But, he found himself all alone in that endeavor. Her brothers both understood her feeling regarding wanting to stay away and be independent.

But, now that spring was upon all of them, they all went back at it hard and fast. She practically moved right into the gym. She did sixteen hours a day once, sometimes twice a week. The other days were at least eight hours, and often more. But, it was a labor of love. It was really beginning to come together. It certainly looked completely different than it had last year.

Then arrived the day for inspection. They called her and told her when to be there. Tom mentioned that he would be leading them but that they were bringing in professional inspectors. There would be someone there to inspect every angle of it: plumbing, electrical, structure, the floors, a locksmith, and others to specify.

Rick said he would be there. She expressed extreme nervousness and fear. But, at the same time, she also felt a peace about it. Tom had proved to be nothing short of supportive this whole year. He did mention, however, that a couple of the board members would also be present. She was a grown woman. She was not their child, and especially not their rag doll to throw around.

On the day of, Tom managed to arrive just shortly before the inspectors. He and the board members with him. Al also showed up and, of course, Rick. He was the early bird. She stuck close to him the whole time. He was glad of it. They were both to receive the brunt of this.

Upon their arrival, they dispersed throughout the inside and outside of the gym. They carried clip boards full of paperwork and tape measures. But, they were the only ones doing anything. All anybody else could do was wait for the inspection to conclude. And that seemed to take hours. But, in reality, it lasted one hour. And, then they were all done.

All that they said was that they would compare notes and render their decision within a week. One of them gave her a card and instructed her to call if she hasn't heard anything back within a week. She though that that was nice of them to do that. She agreed and they all left out pleasantly enough.

What a week! She thought and hoped…and prayed. There was minimal work this week and more time to work out. Her and went out and when they were finished, kissed good-night. An incredible peace came over her. She relished in the ease of it at this point. Al called a couple of times to see if she had heard anything.

But it didn't take a week, more like five days. She got a call from the City Clerk's office. They said she needed to come down to sign some papers. It was an official act. She called both Rick and Al. She even called Tom.

They all said "Go for it!"

The drive over proved nothing but a big smile, and one short shout of triumph.

She arrived there and the clerk sat down with her in front of some papers. In front of the clerk on the desk, she could read the writing on it was the license to run the gym. She couldn't wait to sign it...and frame it. There would be a party. God was good! She was fantastically amazed.

She signed the license, shook the clerk's hand, and set out immediately to have it framed. She went out to lunch with Rick and took it to the mission to show Al. He nodded and he hugged her. They all agreed there'd have to be a party. So, they planned it, at the gym of course. They would do it that Friday night.

A whole lot of people came out Friday. The place was full. Tom was there. Rick and his dad were, no bowling this Friday. Bob Alice brought the kids. And a whole lot of others showed up as well. She even gave a speech. It was short, but sweet. She thanked a lot of people.

After her speech, she spotted Al. He was, once again, in deep thought. So, she came over and offered him the standard penny his thoughts. He chuckled and sat down in a chair. She sat down next to him. He thought for a minute and looked at her. His mind seemed troubled at that moment.

CONCLUSION

His mind was indeed troubled. So, with the assurance of leaving the mission in capable hands, he took a sabbatical. He went away for healing from memories of a childhood trauma. Thinking errors had emerged causing mixed up emotions of fear and anger. He needed time to talk with someone who could lend a professional and objective ear. He found just that and could finally live in peace with turning his will and his life over to the care of God. In time he would remarry and his relationship with his daughter would be restored.

Printed in the United States
By Bookmasters